A Clerical Error

A Yellow Cottage Vintage Mystery Book 3

J. NEW

Cover Illustration – William Webb

Typography – Coverkicks

Copyright © 2018

Chapter ONE

THE MAY DAY CELEBRATIONS on Linhay were as much a part of island life as the tides themselves, and the undercurrent of excitement as arrangements were made was almost palpable. However, my first attendance at the festivities, in nineteen thirty-six, was memorable for all the wrong reasons; for that was the year a particularly nasty murder occurred.

To make matters worse my own life was unravelling in ways I could never have envisaged, and my worry would begin to overshadow the investigation when it came. With the luxury of hindsight it took me longer than normal to realise the importance of certain clues.

Starting with a telephone call from my husband John, whom I had been told had died, it had become apparent that everything I had believed for the last two years was a lie, including the role of my housekeeper Mrs Shaw.

Just over a week after the call, still smarting from a combination of embarrassment and fury at what had come to light since, and with the feeling of claustrophobia threatening to overwhelm, I decided a change of scenery was needed and made plans to spend the week with Aunt Margaret.

I said goodbye to my gardener Tom, who was hard at work unearthing the Victorian walled garden we had discovered some weeks earlier, and took a taxi to the station. Mrs Shaw was under strict instructions to telephone me at my aunt's immediately if there was news. I had been seated in my train carriage for only a few minutes when suddenly there was a shrill whistle, and a loud hiss of steam came billowing along the platform and past my window moments later, then with a jolt we started slowly forward and gradually picked up speed. Within minutes the station was left behind, then the city suburbs rushed past and before long we were moving into open country. I settled back in my seat and replayed the conversation I'd had a few days ago with the Home Secretary...

"Are you telling me John is in fact still alive?" I asked with barely suppressed fury and the threatening sting of tears behind my eyes.

He paused looking extremely uncomfortable. Eventually he leaned back and sighed.

"We're not sure, I'm afraid he's gone missing. This telephone call you received is the first indication we've had in months he may still be alive."

"What do you mean he's gone missing? He was supposed to be dead. I don't understand anything you're saying."

"I think you'd better tell her everything from the beginning, old chap. She deserves to know the truth," said Uncle Albert, who had accompanied Lord Carrick.

Albert wasn't strictly my uncle, but was Godfather to my sister-in-law Ginny. He was also the Police Commissioner at Scotland Yard, and I had worked closely with him on two previous murder inquiries. It was at his recommendation I had been employed as a consultant detective.

"Yes, you're right of course, I apologise, Miss Bridges. The fact of the matter is John was recruited to MI5 directly upon graduating from Oxford. This was prior to his meeting and marrying you of course. He turned out to be an exceptional operative, one of our best in fact."

"So he was a spy all along?" I asked.

Lord Carrick gave a curt nod.

"He was fluent in several languages, which of course made him a valuable asset."

I was astonished at that news.

"I had no idea. It looks as though I didn't know my husband at all," I said lamely.

I clasped my hands until my knuckles turned white, as a wave of cold spread through my body and I began to shiver. I felt quite sick and fought to suppress the feeling of nausea as Lord Carrick continued.

"You saw what you expected to see. John was a trained undercover operative and there was no reason for you to suspect he was anything other than what he claimed. But if it's any consolation I think you knew the real him better than anyone."

"I'm sorry, but I don't find it in the least bit consoling, the man I thought was my husband was in fact a total stranger. I can't think why he married me in the first place."

"He married you because he fell in love with you, it's as simple as that. We tried to talk him out of it of course; the type of work he was doing was dangerous and having a family makes it all the more difficult. We encourage our men to remain single in fact but, John was insistent and rather than lose him we relented."

"So what happened to him?"

"Please understand I am bound by the Official Secrets Act so am not at liberty to divulge everything. However, I will tell you what I can. John was one of the best undercover men we had as I said, and he was used extensively to infiltrate organisations abroad and send back information we needed."

"What sort of information?"

"I'm afraid I can't tell you that. But suffice to say he was very successful. During his last mission..."

"Where exactly was his last mission?"

"Germany. And just so you understand, it was indeed to be his last assignment. He'd formally put in for retirement from active overseas duties as he wanted to spend more time at home. With you. Unfortunately things didn't go according to plan and we lost communication with him. He missed several rendezvous then disappeared from the radar completely. It's thought his cover had been blown."

"You mean he was taken prisoner?"

"We're not sure. I'm afraid the intelligence is somewhat lacking, but it's assumed so, yes."

I was simply stunned and was finding it difficult to formulate simple questions, as though my head were stuffed with cotton. I felt the prick of tears as I realised John had intended to retire and come home so we could begin a normal life together. I'd had no idea, yet his plans were derailed at the last moment by some dastardly quirk of fate. I swallowed past the lump in my throat and the rising bile; it was all so unfair.

"So you assumed whoever took him had him killed? You told me at the time he was shot accidentally on a farm in India and that he didn't suffer at all. I take it this was not actually the case considering what I know now?"

"Well the body..."

"What about the body? Two years ago you identified it as my husband. You came to my home and told me he was dead and gave me his wedding ring. If my husband is dead, Lord Carrick, then just how is it he telephoned me last evening?"

Lord Carrick rose and approached the fire. Leaning on the mantel he stared into the flames and began to talk softly, almost to himself.

"The news came in that a body had been found in the early hours. One of our chaps happened to be in the area at the time and went to investigate. What he found was the body of a man, charred beyond recognition, in the lower level of a factory which was still partially burning. We know now it was arson used to cover up a murder; the victim had been shot. Naturally our man quickly searched the body for any means of identification, but the only thing he found was the wedding ring. He removed it, then left the scene. There was nothing more he could do; he was putting himself at great risk as it was. Because the ring was engraved it was naturally assumed the body belonged to your husband, it was his ring after all."

"But now you don't think it was?" I asked.

He glanced at me quickly but didn't answer my question.

"A couple of months ago we received a report citing the possibility John had been spotted in the company of some high level German officials, but before it could be confirmed he disappeared. Naturally we've been searching for him ever since but to no avail."

I shot out of my chair before I had a chance to think about what I was doing.

"You mean to say you knew my husband was alive two months ago and didn't tell me? How dare you keep this from me? Dear God, what sort of people are you?"

"Miss Bridges, please understand we couldn't confirm anything. We didn't know whether it was your husband or someone who simply bore a striking resemblance to him. Remember, in these situations John would be in disguise. It would have been remiss, no, it would have been cruel of me to come to you then only to find out it wasn't him."

I sat down at the end of this little speech and put my

head in my hands, all the fight had left me. My skin felt cold and clammy, and along with the shakes, which were getting worse, my heart was beating wildly. I felt a hand on my shoulder and looked up to see the blurry shape of Albert hovering over me, a large brandy in his hand. So mired was I in my own thoughts I hadn't even heard him move.

"Drink this, Ella, you've had a nasty shock."

I nodded, and taking a large gulp immediately felt the warmth of the liquid suffuse my body, and the anxiousness abate somewhat, though not entirely. John was alive. It was almost too much to believe after all this time, but in my heart I knew it was true. I felt a surge of hope course through my veins as I asked Lord Carrick for confirmation. I needed to hear him say it out loud.

"But now you think it was him because he telephoned me?"

"Yes, and we're doing everything within our power to find him."

"And bring him home? You must bring him home, it's much too dangerous for him there."

My emotions were vacillating between elation that John was alive, and abject fear of the peril he was in. The thought I would lose him again forever was simply unbearable.

"We're doing everything we can to find him, Miss Bridges, and as soon as I know anything I will come and speak with you. However, please be aware it may not be a simple job to extract him. If the reports we've received are true then he a magnificent vista of verdant lawns and topiary hedges. Inside, giant ferns, orange trees and rare orchids vied for space with several more exotic varieties for which I had no name, and to the right a comfortable seating area and low table had been set for tea.

I threw myself in a chair and breathed a sigh of relief.

"Now, Ella, I realise you couldn't speak on the telephone but I sensed in your voice something was wrong, and I can see now you've lost some weight. What on earth has happened?"

"Oh, Aunt Margaret, it appears John is still alive," I wailed, and to my absolute horror I promptly burst into tears.

"Good heavens! Well, that's the last thing I expected you to say. You go ahead and have a good cry, dear girl. Personally I feel all this British stiff upper lip malarkey is perfect nonsense. I find one always feels much better when one can let it all out as it were."

As usual Aunt Margaret was correct. Once the sobs had subsided and the pent up emotion released I did feel better.

"Now dry your eyes, dear, and tell me what you know."

I began with the shock of the phone call, then related subsequent events as they had happened, including the conversation with Lord Carrick.

"So John is in Germany?" Aunt Margaret asked.

"As far as is known, yes, but it seems he's vanished."

She sighed and took my hand in hers.

"I'll not beat about the bush, Ella, that's not my way as you know, but there is rumour of another world war, one with Germany at the heart of it."

I gasped. "How do you know?"

"You don't reach my age without knowing a bit about the world, darling. Plus I have friends in high places. However I don't want you to worry too much, it is just a rumour and may never happen."

"But I do worry, Aunt Margaret. How can I not when John is in so much danger?"

"Oh, darling, I feel for you I truly do, but if anyone knows exactly what's going on, far more than my friends I hasten to add, it's John. He's there and knows first-hand their intentions. Whether it comes to war or not it's John's job to ensure our government is kept abreast of what is happening. It's an exceptionally important job he's doing."

I stood up and went to gaze out of the window, my mind in turmoil at my aunt's revelation there may be another war. I wondered where John was and what he was doing at that moment. Was he thinking of me as I was thinking of him?

"Did you know John was a spy? I seem to remember you weren't really taken with him when I brought him home that first time."

"Then you remember incorrectly, Ella. I liked him very much and thought him perfect for you. However, to answer your question, no, I didn't know his job was espionage but I felt he was being a little circumspect with the truth. Not

"Ah, I see."

"Can you believe they intercepted my post?"

"Of course I can, Ella, this is the Government we're talking about, normal rules don't apply."

"Well, they should," I said in a petulant voice and was rewarded with a raised eyebrow. I sighed. "Don't do that Aunt Margaret."

"Do what dear?"

"Make me feel guilty."

"I'm doing no such thing, that's your conscience talking."

"You'd be furious in my position too. My freedom of choice was removed, not to mention my privacy. The sheer audacity of these people astounds me."

"Well, correct me if I'm wrong, but I believe it was all done in order to protect you?"

"But I don't need protection. I've already had to change back to my maiden name and move miles away from our home. I did everything the Home Secretary advised but it still wasn't enough, so they ensconced a charlatan in my home under false pretenses. It's appalling behaviour."

"Goodness me, Ella, if you keep this up I'll have no choice but to send you to bed without any supper."

I glanced at her, spied the smirk and the twinkle in her eye.

"Yes, all right, point taken. But I'm still furious and I don't know what to do about Mrs Shaw, if indeed that's her name."

"What do you mean 'do?'"

"Well I can hardly keep her on as my housekeeper now, I can barely bring myself to talk to her."

"Ella, that's simply dreadful behaviour, rather like shooting the messenger. The poor woman is just doing her job, following orders actually. How would you feel in her position?"

That brought me up short. Remarkably I hadn't considered things from Mrs Shaw's point of view and I was rather ashamed of the fact. Emotion and shock had obviously clouded my normally sound judgment. I resolved to speak with her as soon as I returned home. It would be a difficult conversation but it had to be done.

"Thank you, Aunt Margaret."

"Think nothing of it, my dear. I feel it always helps to speak to someone on the periphery as it were, it brings things into perspective. And there's no need to feel guilty, Ella, you're perfectly entitled to have a tantrum now and again, particularly as the root cause is worry about John. Just so long as you don't make a habit of it."

I smiled. "There's no need to worry on that score, Aunt Margaret. Admittedly it's all a bit of a mare's nest, but there's really very little I can do now except wait, and hope," and worry, I silently added to myself.

"And keep yourself busy," my aunt added. "There's nothing worse than sitting around brooding and worrying. Now, there's been a couple of additions to the town since you were here last, a perfectly lovely milliners and a delightful tea room close to the Guild Hall. My treat."

True to her word, I departed The Lilly Tea Rooms stuffed to the gills, which was an immense change compared to recent days where I pushed food around my plate and barely ate a morsel. My appetite had all but disappeared since I'd heard from John, and I was definitely a few pounds lighter if my loose skirt was anything to go by. But I'd always been a little overweight so could afford the loss.

My aunt took me to the milliner's, where I left with a thoroughly practical and sensible new hat in dove grey with a button detail. Although it would have been quite a different story had I let the shop girl have her way.

"I'm so very relieved you didn't choose that first hat, Ella," Aunt Margaret said, laughing.

"The one with all the feathers you mean? Goodness, while I appreciate the artistry, I would have been too afraid of wearing it lest I be shot at."

Laughing at my near escape we wandered companionably down the High Street through the bustling crowds, and I was pleased to note the clouds I had been worried about earlier had almost disappeared. In their place a hazy sunshine was valiantly attempting to cast its rays down to street level.

We stopped periodically to peer in shop windows if a particular item caught our eye, and it was in front of the newly established delicatessen, where an impressive range of French cheeses were on display, that my aunt remembered her recent correspondence. My mother had moved to the South of France, and judging from her periodic letters and postcards, was having a perfectly wonderful time.

"I received a letter from your mother a couple of days ago, it seems she's caught the interest of a retired British Colonel out there and he's making gallant attempts to woo her, much to her amusement."

"Really? Is it serious do you think?"

"Oh, I doubt it, well certainly not on your mother's part, although heaven knows how the Colonel feels. He's probably smitten; men usually are around your mother you know."

"Well, I'm sure she knows what she's doing and will let him down gently if needs be."

"I expect you're right, Ella. Now what do you say we enter this fine establishment? I've recently been gifted a rather superior port, which is crying out for a special accompaniment."

Twenty minutes later, my aunt having purchased enough cheese to feed the Foreign Legion and the British Army combined, we exited the shop and continued to the end of the street, where I was expertly steered left in the direction of a small art gallery. I knew the gallery existed, but had never visited during the times I had lived with my aunt.

"Are you of a mind to purchase a painting, Aunt Margaret?" I asked, as we crossed the road.

"Not at present, dear. Although it has been known for me to leave this particular gallery with a piece I didn't know I wanted," she said with a laugh. "Now tell me, what do you think?"

I gazed at the artwork on display in the window.

"Well, art isn't normally my bailiwick, Aunt Margaret, I feel it's quite subjective. I find I like things because of what they are as opposed to what is deemed fashionable."

"Quite right too."

"But he does have an accomplished hand, and a unique style."

I gazed at the pictures in the window, each one a depiction of hard northern life painted in monochrome. Men in large overcoats and flat caps slogged up cobbled roads on their way to work, huge old factories in the background, grey and dull, belched smoke into the atmosphere, the plumes rising to join the miasma of fog overhead.

Urchins playing in the street in boots too big for their feet and rags barely covering their skeletal frames looked out with huge eyes and cheeky grins. While mothers, babes on their hips and toddlers grasping at their skirts, stared defiantly out of the canvas, proud and strangely regal despite their reduced circumstances. They were a peculiar combination of dispiriting and uplifting, and I found I liked them. One, an impish little girl, reminded me of my very first case at an orphanage in London, and unexpectedly I felt a pang at the family John and I had thus far missed out on.

There was one painting, however, tucked into the bottom right hand corner as though it were an afterthought to place it on display, which I disliked immediately. Unlike the others it was bright and colourful, and at first glance it appeared to be an image of a beautiful young woman sitting on a park bench with an old church in the background. On closer inspection however she appeared to be a woman of two halves.

It was remarkably well done, and was testament to the prowess of the artist that I had such a visceral response to it. The left side of her face was perfect in every way, from the rich cornflower blue of her long lashed eye, the finely arched brow and the rosebud pink of her smiling mouth, she appeared happy and carefree. A woman who was selfless, an open book and one you'd be glad to call a friend. But with a few clever strokes of the brush the right side was transformed. The eye became malevolent with a hard glint suggesting an underlying animosity, the mouth a sneer as though full of contempt for the viewer and above the top lip an ugly and exaggerated black mole grew, as though the rottenness of the core were attempting to burst through the skin. I gave an involuntary shiver, as though evil had crossed my path and glanced at the title, 'From Mistress to Wife.'

I straightened and looked at Aunt Margaret with a raised brow.

"Very clever, isn't it?" she said.

"Undoubtedly. But I can't say I like it, and I find I'm hard pushed to believe anyone in their right mind would want to hang it on their wall."

She laughed. "Come along, let's go in."

I followed her into the shop and smiled as I glimpsed a black cat, wearing a purple collar with a silver bell, curled up asleep in the window.

"Terribly flattering," she replied.

Having completed his inspection of my physique and deemed me becoming, but rather on the heavy side to be fashionable, he strode forward to face me.

"So what is it you do, ma chére?"

"Do?" I asked, nonplussed for a moment.

"Yes 'do,'" he repeated in an exasperated tone. "What are your interests, your hobbies? What are your hopes and dreams?"

I frowned. "As a matter of fact I am a consultant detective with Scotland Yard."

The small man clutched his chest and staggered back, eyes wide as though he'd been shot.

"Oh my gawd, you're 'avin a larf, ain't ya?"

I raised an eyebrow in surprise. "Obviously not as much as you are Mr...?"

"Oh dear, well that's rather let the cat out of the bag," Aunt Margaret said. "Ella, I'd like to introduce you to the world renowned artist, Monsieur Pierre DuPont. Formerly known as Norman Sprout, master forger of Brick Lane, London."

"Maggie, I can't believe you've brought a copper to me door, after all we've been through," said the thoroughly dejected artist. He moved to the chaise-longue and sat with his head in his hands.

"Oh, stop being so melodramatic, Norman, I've done no such thing. Ella happens to be my niece and is currently taking a few days holiday to visit her old aunt."

"What, so you mean you're not the old bill?"

"I'm exactly what I told you, Mr Sprout, I'm not in the habit of lying. However, unless you have an inclination to murder your customers I doubt our paths will cross in a professional capacity."

"Murder! Gordon Bennet, Maggie, what is this? I ain't never murdered anyone in me life! I'm just a simple artist tryin' to earn a crust. All right, I admit I started on the wrong side of the tracks, but I've been straight as an arrow ever since that incident with The Duke of Bainbridge and 'Desdemona with Sheep.'"

I raised a quizzical eyebrow.

"It's a painting, dear," Aunt Margaret explained. "A long story and I won't bore you with the details, but it's how Norman and I met. And, Norman, do you really think after all this time, not to mention the investment, I would do anything to jeopardise our friendship?"

"Oh, Maggie, please forgive me, I wasn't thinkin' straight."

"No matter, I shall put it down to artistic temperament. However if you are as you say, 'on the straight and narrow,' I do believe your reaction was a little over the top, don't you?"

Norman sighed and rose to his feet shaking his head.

"Only I could have gone into partnership with the cleverest woman in Christendom."

Partnership? This was certainly news to me and I glanced at my aunt in wonder. There was obviously a lot I didn't know.

"There's been rumours," continued Norman. "Come on,

"Desdemona with Sheep?" I hazarded a guess.

"Quite right," confirmed my aunt. "It's a very famous painting by the Dutch master, Johannes Van-der Bleck, and quite priceless. So the duke and I quietly made our way to the gallery so as not to arouse suspicion, and once there we were greeted by the sight of dear Pierre, or Norman as he was then, halfway up a curtain and clinging on for dear life, while one of the duke's dogs stood guard below."

"It was the size of a horse!" said Pierre, shuddering at the memory.

"It was a Pomeranian," corrected my aunt. "Of course I could see immediately he was innocent."

Pierre chuckled and shook his head.

"Only Maggie could have seen my innocence while in that predicament. I'd been caught halfway out of the window, my rope was still in place, my tools were in a bag on the floor and the spoils were at my feet. I'd been caught red-handed and it was only a matter of time before the police arrived and I was thrown in a cell."

"But however did you manage to escape?" I asked.

My Aunt once again took up the narrative.

"Oh, he didn't need to escape. As I said before he was entirely innocent, not that the duke thought so. Of course a discreet word in his ear about certain matters soon had him seeing my point of view."

"You mean to say you blackmailed him?" I asked in astonishment.

"Of course not. I just gently reminded him of the incident between his son, a local tavern maid and Lord Ellesmere's prize race horse. I'd been instrumental in keeping it quiet, you see. But of course that's a story for another time. Back to Desdemona."

Pierre rose at this point and collected the tea things.

"I'll leave your aunt to explain while I make more tea."

"That reminds me, why on earth are you playing housemaid?" asked my Aunt. "Where's that girl of yours?"

"Hilda? It's her day off. Why do you suppose you found me in the shop and not in the studio."

When Pierre had gone I asked Aunt Margaret to explain how she knew immediately he was innocent of the crime when all evidence said otherwise.

"Well you see, Ella, the duke and I had been friends for a long time and I had visited the gallery on many occasions. It was on one such visit that I realised the painting in question was actually a rather masterful forgery. Goodness knows how long it had hung there without anyone noticing, rather a long time I suspect. The duke had grown up in that house, you see, and had passed through the gallery numerous times. It's amazing when you see something every day for years just how little notice you take of it, it becomes nothing more than background."

"So Pierre had actually stolen a forgery?"

"Goodness me, no. Pierre can spot a forgery a mile away, it was his stock-in-trade at the time. No, the original was hanging in its rightful place on the wall. That's how I knew he was innocent."

I sat back in amazement as it all became clearer.

"But why on earth would he go to all the trouble of replacing a forgery with the original, knowing he may be caught? And who painted the forgery? And for that matter who stole the original in the first place?"

"Oh, Isobella, so many questions," my aunt said, patting my knee. "I doubt we'll ever know the answers."

I doubted that was the case but knew better than to pursue it, I would get nothing more from Aunt Margaret.

"So you became his benefactor."

"I did."

"A known art thief, forger and criminal?" I said in wonder.

"In my experience the world is very rarely black and white, but instead various shades of grey. Norman needed my help and I gave it to him. And not once have I ever regretted the decision. Ah now, here's the tea."

"But how did the duke explain it all to his butler?" I asked, rising to take the tray from Pierre.

"Oh, something about a test designed to find any flaws in the security. Everyone went away with a pat on the back and a hefty bonus. Now be an angel and pass me some of that delectable looking cake."

I poured the tea and cut the fruit cake while Pierre explained the rumours he'd mentioned previously.

"As your aunt knows, the professional art world is remarkably small, Miss Bridges, and the underside of that world even more so. I keep my ear to the ground and hear various murmurings, and once in a while I am contacted by a most trusted confidante for information. He contacted me last week to ask if I'd heard anything about a British gang targeting the French. Apparently there are plans afoot to attempt the most audacious of crimes, a theft from the Louvre."

"My goodness!" exclaimed my Aunt. "And what have you heard, Pierre? I can't for one moment imagine how they expect to succeed in such an endeavour; the Louvre is as well guarded as the Crown Jewels."

"I agree, Maggie. It would take an exceptional mind to pull off that particular job and the risks are high. In my opinion it's impossible. As to what I've heard, well that is even more peculiar, for I have heard nothing at all. The grapevine is deathly silent."

"Well, wouldn't that indicate your chap has got it wrong?" I asked.

Pierre stroked his graying goatee absentmindedly and nodded slowly. "That is possibly so. But I shall keep my ear to the ground and make some discreet inquiries nonetheless."

I continued to sip my tea while Pierre and my aunt discussed the art world. I knew little of it myself, which is undoubtedly why I didn't realise how important my meeting with Pierre would turn out to be. Not only with regard to the imminent murder inquiry, but also to a worrying telephone conversation

I would soon have with my mother.

In the excitement of the conversation both my aunt and I had lost track of the time, and it was late afternoon when we left.

On the way out Pierre stopped me.

"How do you think of my work, Meez Bridges?" he asked, once again reverting to his impeccable French accent.

"As a matter of fact I said to Aunt Margaret earlier how much I liked it. Well, apart from one that is."

"Oh? And which one is it that you do not care for?"

"I'm afraid the one of the woman in the window isn't much to my liking. It's a personal choice, you understand, the work itself is exceptionally good but the subject matter just doesn't appeal I'm afraid. I hope I haven't offended you?"

"Oh, but of course not. You are the niece of Maggie, no? So all is well. If you had been any other though? Pfft! Who knows? But what is this painting, I cannot place it?"

"The two-faced woman."

"Mon Dieu! Theese should not be in the window! It is the fault of the idiotic Hilda, no doubt. It shall be removed at once."

He hurried to the display, removed the offending painting and deposited it deftly behind the curtain.

"There, order and beauty is once again restored," he said

with a smile, which didn't quite mask the panic in his eyes. "Now I shall bestow upon you a gift, Ella."

"Oh, there's really no need."

"I insist. Now stand there and do not move so much as an inch, there is something most perfect here for you. I shall know it when I see it."

My aunt smiled at me, and moving aside a painting of a boy throwing a stick for a small scruffy dog, sat on the chaise-longue to wait.

"You'd better do as he says, dear, there's no talking him out of it."

So I stood patiently while Pierre ran up and down ladders with amazing agility looking for the perfect piece. Every so often Aunt Margaret and I shared a smile as the small man muttered, "No, not this one," and "Oh thees will never do," but eventually it seemed the perfect painting was indeed found.

"Aha! Thees is the one."

He scurried down the ladder, approached me, and with a flourish presented me with a small painting approximately ten inches square in a gilt frame. I gasped when I saw it was a beautiful rendition of a small urchin girl sitting on a stoop with a black cat on her knee. I eyed Monsieur Dupont closely. He couldn't possibly know I could see spirits, yet this was the second time he had intimated he knew of my unusual way of seeing the world. Nor could he know I had a black ghost cat, yet his prescience at choosing such a remarkably apt painting was uncanny, and I wondered if there was more to this diminutive little man than I had first thought.

"Thank you, Pierre, it is perfect, as you knew it would be. It appears I am not the only one who views the world differently."

Pierre inclined his head in agreement, and with eyes twinkling in amusement deftly wrapped the picture for me to take. I already knew the perfect place to hang it once I returned to the cottage.

With promises to meet again soon, my aunt and I left Monsieur DuPont to what remained of his day and continued back up the high street to Carnaby's Tea Emporium, from whence, armed with several dark green and gold boxes emblazoned with the Carnaby name, we caught a taxi back home.

Chapter TWO

THE FEW DAYS I SPENT with Aunt Margaret were exactly what I needed to restore my equilibrium, and prevent my mind from dwelling on matters over which I had no control. She had kept me busy and entertained throughout the week, but all too soon our time together came to an end. However in her usual show of intuition she detected my slight trepidation in returning to the cottage.

"Now, Ella, as you know I have been meaning to visit you on Linhay as soon as time allowed, and as it turns out I have some free time toward the end of the month. Mrs Shipley has informed me her church has cancelled the usual fundraiser this year, therefore my managerial skills are not needed. I never used to attend of course, you know my views on organised religion."

"So why help if you don't believe?" I asked.

"I didn't say I don't believe; however, my housekeeper believes and that's all that matters. Besides the building is old

Chapter THREE

THE REMAINDER OF THE WEEK flew by as Mrs Shaw and I settled down to writing 'The Compendium of Ways it is possible for an officer of the law to tell when a suspect is lying', but it was proving difficult to explain by words alone. I also needed to think of a much snappier title.

"I think it would benefit from having pictures," said Mrs Shaw glumly, after we had attempted to write a particularly stubborn paragraph in three different ways.

"An excellent idea, Mrs Shaw, I don't know why I didn't think of it. I may know of someone who would be perfect for the job too."

After a quick telephone call to leave a message at Scotland Yard I returned to Mrs Shaw.

"I think we'll call it a day. I have the meeting for the Fete Committee shortly and I need to eat something before I go."

"I believe Mrs Parsons has left something in the kitchen for you."

At Mrs Shaw's request, Mrs Parsons had agreed to come in three mornings a week until I found someone permanent.

"What with looking after him indoors and still cleaning up at the hotel, I can't promise more than that, Miss Bridges. I am sorry."

I assured her it was perfectly all right, and I appreciated her help during the interim.

"If you know of anyone who is looking for such work, do let me know," I said.

I ate my dinner at my desk and half an hour later was ready to leave. Mrs Shaw had volunteered to drop me off and wait for me.

"We have a motor car at our disposal, Miss Bridges, we may as well use it."

I was through the lych-gate and had just started to wend my way up the church path when a breathless voice called out behind me. It was Agnes.

"Hello, Ella. Gosh, it's a chilly breeze this evening, isn't it? I do so hope they've managed to fix the boiler otherwise it will be a very short meeting. Actually I'm glad I caught you. I have some news. Do you remember that woman who bumped into to you the other day? Well I've found out who she is."

"I didn't realise you were looking for her," I said.

"Oh, I wasn't really, it was purely by chance. I was just

utes I left them to play and reached the other side unscathed.

"Good morning, Ella. How are you and your aunt getting on?" asked Agnes.

"Oh, we've finished setting up now, just waiting for the customers."

"Well, there's already a huge crowd outside the gate and several charabancs queuing to drop off their passengers. There's obviously a few work outings been planned for today. You'll need to have your wits about you when the gate opens as there's always a rush for your stall."

"I'm not surprised. There's some lovely pieces, my aunt and I have already purchased some. Is that raspberry preserve I spy there?"

"It is, mother and I make it. And this one is apple and ginger. Would you like some?"

"I would indeed, could you put one of each aside for me? I'd better take some of that red onion chutney too, it's a favourite of my aunt's. Jocasta, are you all right?" I asked, spying her behind the horticulture.

She was sitting in a deck chair behind her stall, fanning herself with a newspaper.

"Truth be told, Ella, I feel quite ghastly. I think I must be running a slight temperature and feel quite nauseous."

"Oh dear, have you caught the same infection Prudence Fielding and Anne have?"

"It certainly looks like it, unfortunately I think Father Michael might be likewise afflicted. He's supposed to be opening the fete today but he looks much worse than I do. He visited Prudence the other day when he heard she was poorly so obviously picked it up then. I do hope he's all right."

"Don't worry, I saw him not five minutes ago heading toward the ribbon. He did look quite flushed and shaky, but he'll not let the side down, especially today," said Agnes.

At that moment we were interrupted by the ringing of the bell.

"That's the signal, it's opening time," announced Jocasta staggering to her feet. "Good luck, girls. Here's to a successful fundraiser."

I most definitely underestimated Agnes's meaning when she said there would be a rush for my stall. Once the gates were open a swarm of humanity surged onto the green and all seemed to be headed in my direction. Before long the table was six deep with everyone jostling for space, grabbing things from the table and thrusting coins into my hands. It was absolute chaos and I can't say I had much control at all in the beginning.

More than once a fight broke out between members of the lower classes who desired the same item and I had to play referee, and twice I caught someone trying to take an item without paying for it. But a stern talking to, a slap on the wrist and the threat of a policeman soon sorted that out. After the third wave of customers had been served and the items replenished, it calmed down to a more manageable pace as people moved on to other vendors and the tea pavilion. I glanced at Aunt Margaret who had been every bit as busy as I had, but seemed much more serene.

"You're very popular today, Miss Bridges, I've been trying to get to see you for the last hour."

"Sergeant Baxter, how lovely to see you. I didn't realise you would be here today."

"I always bring the missus here for the May Day celebrations, take a room at a lovely little boarding house on the front for a couple of days. It's run by the wife's sister, Elsie Pennyworth. Mrs Baxter deserves a bit of a holiday after putting up with me all year."

The sergeant and I had first met during the case up at Arundel Hall, and I had been very taken with his artistic ability. He was a very nice man and an astute policeman who was highly regarded by his boss, the Chief of Police Sir Albert Montesford, who also happened to be Ginny's Godfather.

"So where is Mrs Baxter?" I asked.

"She's gone to have tea with Elsie. Actually I wanted to have a word about the message you left at The Yard the other day."

"Yes, the illustrations for the compendium? Mrs Shaw and I have agreed it would be far more useful to illustrate the points and of course I immediately thought of you. I wondered if you would be agreeable to providing drawings? You would be paid for your time of course."

"I think that would be right up my street, Miss Bridges, I'd be honoured. Do you have time to have a chat over a cup of tea and a bun?"

"That's a very good idea, I'm quite parched myself."

After Aunt Margaret had agreed to hold the fort at both our stalls, Sergeant Baxter and I made our way to the pavilion. It was lovely and cool inside and it looked very inviting with its crisp white tablecloths and large potted palms. We were guided to a recently vacated table just inside the entrance by a smart waitress, who took our order and informed us it would be along shortly. We were lucky to have found a table as nearly all the others were full. I spied the vicar on the next one over talking to an elderly parishioner. Jocasta was right he didn't look well at all, and I noticed him constantly mopping his sweating brow with his handkerchief.

"I'll just go next door and let Mrs Baxter know where I am."

By 'next door' he meant the section beyond the bank of greenery reserved for the less genteel clientele. It was situated nearer to the bandstand, and while the string quartet behind me were exceptionally good, the lively rendition of 'Knees up Mother Brown' coming from that direction signalled a much more fun time was being had by all.

"She and Elsie are fine, having a lovely catch up and a bit of a sing song as you can no doubt hear," Baxter said with a sheepish smile.

"I was just thinking what fun it must be. You're sure you don't want to join them, it is your holiday after all?"

"I've only ever sung once in my life, Miss Bridges, and that was..."

But I never found out when it was, as a resounding crash from the next table had me jumping from my seat. Father Michael had collapsed, taking the tablecloth and the crockery with him.

Chapter FOUR

I RUSHED OVER AND CROUCHING next to the fallen vicar, felt for a pulse. Leaning back I glanced at Baxter and whispered.

"I'm afraid your holiday is to be cut short, Sergeant Baxter. Father Michael is quite dead."

Neither Sergeant Baxter nor myself could hazard a guess at what had befallen the vicar, but both of us agreed it was suspicious. Therefore we came to a mutual understanding, we would treat everything as though a crime had taken place until we knew otherwise.

Baxter immediately took charge of the situation, sending a runner to find the doctor and commandeering several constables, who had initially been seconded from the force on the mainland to deal with crowd control, to guard the pavilion and prevent anyone from leaving. He cordoned off the immediate area surrounding the body and saw that the tea paraphernalia was collected properly.

"Oh, Ella, thank goodness, I've just heard a rumour that someone has collapsed. Do you know anything?" Agnes asked.

"I'll explain in a minute. First, do you know where Father Michael went on his Sabbatical?"

"Well yes, but what does that have to do...?"

Her eyes widened as she made the connection.

"Has Father Michael collapsed? Is he all right?"

Seeing the distress of her friend Jocasta came over.

"Ella, what's happened?"

I took Agnes's hands in my own and looked her in the eye.

"Agnes, just answer my question, it's important. Did the father travel abroad recently?"

"Abroad? No. I don't think he's ever been abroad in his life, has he, Jocasta? He gets terribly seasick and doesn't trust aeroplanes. He went to York. The Archbishop is a long-time friend, they went to seminary school together, I believe. Now please, tell us what's happened."

I left a shocked Jocasta comforting a distraught Agnes and took a quick detour to bring my Aunt up to date.

"Well, that is tragic news, and such a shock. I suppose considering his age it must be treated as suspicious but I do hope there is a simple explanation. Let me know if I can help in any way, dear."

"Actually I wondered if you'd start to pack up the stalls? There's barely anything left anyway and in light of what's happened..."

"Consider it done. I spied Mrs Shaw a few minutes ago. I'll commandeer her to assist. What happens to the surplus goods?"

"I've no idea. I assume they'd go back to Jocasta as she's the organiser."

"I'll go and speak with her and Miss Shepherd, I daresay they are at sixes and sevens."

I thanked her, gave her a peck on the cheek and returned to Doctor Wenhope. Having given him the news that a quarantine was unnecessary I met with Sergeant Baxter and brought him up to date.

"I never thought of quarantine. A relief it weren't necessary, it would have been a nightmare to sort out today, what with the crowds and suchlike."

"It would indeed, Sergeant. Can you imagine the riot we'd have had on our hands if we had tried to put some of the upper classes in isolation?"

"I shudder to think of it, Miss Bridges, I really do. Well, I'd better get on overseeing this lot."

"I need to assist with packing up the stalls. I'll meet you back here when I'm finished."

"Righto."

Aunt Margaret, Mrs Shaw and I worked quickly and efficiently, but it still took an hour and a half to pack everything away and carry it all to the motor car. By the time I returned to Baxter I found he'd concluded his investigations and was placing the last of the samples in a box ready for transport.

"Well, I think we've done all we can here, Miss Bridges. Samples of all the victuals have been taken and labeled, witness statements and contact details obtained and the scene gone over with a fine-tooth comb. I've also practically filled my notebook with sketches and observations."

"Apologies for not being on hand to help," I said. "But very well done, Baxter. If it does turn out to be something other than natural causes we're in jolly good shape to investigate. Ah, here come the ambulance men."

We stood aside as the St John's ambulance volunteers covered the body and wheeled him away to an awaiting vehicle.

"Well, Sergeant Baxter, I don't think there is much more we can do here so I'll take my leave. I think it's time I took my aunt home. What are your plans?"

"I'll collect Mrs Baxter and see her and Elsie safely back, then I'll return to London. It's best if I'm on hand for the results then I can pass 'em straight on to you."

"Will you inform Uncle Albert?"

"I will, 'though I doubt there's much he can do. He's away in Oxfordshire at present, so it'll be up to us to pursue matters if needed."

"I see. Well, let us hope nothing criminal has occurred. Goodbye, Sergeant Baxter."

"Goodbye, Miss Bridges. I'll telephone as soon as I have news."

Aunt Margaret had informed me all the surplus items from the stalls needed to go back to the meeting room. She had passed over our funds and obtained a key from Jocasta who told us she would follow on as soon as she could. So with the car packed, Mrs Shaw drove us back up the hill to St. Mary's.

We left Aunt Margaret in the car. She would never admit it but I could see she was tired from the day's exertions. Having safely returned the unsold items to the meeting room, we were making our way back down the churchyard path when I caught a movement out of the corner of my eye. Turning, I saw the same elderly gentleman dressed in tweeds as I had on my first visit. I raised a hand to wave but he turned and walked through the solid perimeter wall. I sighed.

"Is something wrong, Miss Bridges?"

I could hardly tell Mrs Shaw what I had seen, so a watered down version of the truth would have to suffice.

"I have a feeling that not all is as it should be, Mrs Shaw. There's a mystery here which needs solving and I may be the only one who can do it."

Mrs Shaw, used to my odd ways now, said nothing and we continued toward the car. At the lych-gate we found Jocasta and Agnes talking with Aunt Margaret.

"Oh, Ella, I just can't believe it. Poor Father Michael," said Agnes.

I handed the keys back to Jocasta, who ironically was beginning to look a little better.

J. New

"I am sorry for your loss. I know I didn't know the father personally but I know how much he meant to the both of you."

"You will tell us as soon as you know anything, won't you?" Jocasta asked.

"We know you're investigating," whispered Agnes.

I looked at them, unsure what to say, but Agnes continued.

"I caught Doctor Wenhope as he was leaving and asked him what his thoughts were. He said he couldn't comment but you should have some information soon. He mentioned Scotland Yard. You will let us know, won't you, Ella?"

"I am sorry to interrupt, dear, but would you mind if we went home? I'm feeling quite weary."

"Yes, of course. I'm sorry, Agnes, Jocasta, but I really must get my aunt back, it's been quite an ordeal for her. I'm sure you understand. Do take care, and once again please accept my condolences."

I took Aunt Margaret's arm, and settled her in the back of the car with a rug over her knees as Mrs Shaw started the engine and pulled away.

"Thank you, Aunt."

"Don't mention it," she said, removing the rug. "I could see what a predicament you were in."

I leant back and closed my eyes.

"I know what you're thinking," she said a moment later.

"I'm not sure you do."

"It must be very difficult to retain friends when one minute you're having afternoon tea and the next you're interrogating them as a suspect."

I opened one eye and looked at her.

"As I thought, definitely part witch."

She laughed. "If you want my advice, Ella, try not to dwell on it too much. The real friends will understand when you explain you cannot discuss an ongoing investigation, and won't press you further. They will also still be around when it's concluded."

"Judicious words indeed," I mumbled, half asleep.

"Of course they are; I'm an old woman who has lived twice as long as you have."

"I'm glad you didn't say wiser."

"I didn't need to, dear."

Chapter FIVE

SEVERAL DAYS PASSED BEFORE I heard from Sergeant Baxter. Life at the cottage had settled into a welcome routine with the three of us working on the police compendium in the morning. Aunt Margaret, who had taught me all I knew, was an invaluable help and we were beginning to make real progress. Then in the afternoon, my aunt and I would venture out for walks or drives around the island if the weather was fine, or settle down to a game of Goof spiel or Mau mau if not. But at the back of my mind always was the death of Father Michael, alongside the continual worry about John.

The news when it came was mixed.

"So there were nothing in any of the food or drink served to Father Michael at the fete to cause his death. In fact nothing unusual were found in the victuals served from the pavilion that day at all," Baxter told me.

"I see. I suppose it is good news from the point of view

of the other patrons," I said. "I also had a word with the doctor before he left the fete, and asked him to inform us if anyone came to his surgery feeling ill who had also taken tea in the pavilion. He's not been in contact so I assume all is well."

"But you're not convinced his death were natural?"

"No I'm not, Sergeant Baxter. There is more to the demise of the vicar than we know, I'm sure of it. But without any evidence there's no proof. Is there anything to report from the post-mortem?"

"I'm sorry to say that news isn't so good. There's a bit of a delay. A combination of staff shortage and a streak of unexplained deaths in the city, which take precedence apparently. The pathologist can't start on our case 'til next week."

"What? But that means it will have been over a week since Father Michael died. Evidence may be lost. Is there nothing you can do to hurry things along?"

"I'm sorry, Miss Bridges, but there isn't. I've already called in a few favours to get the lab to run tests based on nothing but a gut feeling..."

"And not even your own gut. I'm sorry, Sergeant, I should know you're doing all you can."

"Well, I've worked with you for a while now, Miss Bridges, and I trust your intuition. Leave it with me; if I can push our case further up the pile then I will. But I can't make any promises. By the way, my superintendent has informed the Diocese. They'll be sending over another priest to run things for a while."

Having thanked Baxter I rang off and returned to my aunt.

"I take it the news wasn't good?" she said, taking one look at my face.

"I suppose it depends on which side you're on. From my side unfortunately not. Sorry to be such a misery, it's just so frustrating. It's not much of a holiday for you, is it? I am sorry, Aunt Margaret."

"Oh, do stop apologising, Ella, you're beginning to sound like Agnes. I'm having a perfectly lovely time, murder aside."

"So you think it was murder too?"

"It doesn't matter what I think, you think it's suspicious and that's enough for me. What we need to do is set our minds to solving the problem."

"I can hardly investigate when there's no proof a crime has been committed. Until we have the post-mortem results giving us a 'yay' or 'nay' to something beastly having happened, my hands are tied. Unfortunately Baxter has just informed me the results will be delayed."

"Well, remember there is more than one way to skin a cat, Ella."

Phantom, who had up until that moment been asleep on hearth rug, raised his head and glared at my aunt with such indignation, I couldn't help but laugh.

"What do you have in mind?" I asked.

"The police force isn't the only organisation in the land which wields power, you know."

"The Church," I said after a moment's thought.

She nodded. "I understood your vicar had some friends in high places, perhaps that would be a place to start?"

Strictly speaking, having not passed this new test I wasn't supposed to drive alone, but I felt a little uncomfortable having Mrs Shaw with me constantly while I was investigating, so I decided I would plead ignorance if I was stopped.

After my aunt's excellent observation my next port of call was to Agnes, in the hope I could obtain information which would expedite matters.

"Ella, come through to the parlour, I'll have Molly make us some tea and then we can talk. Mother is resting so we should be left alone for a while," Agnes said in her hushed tone.

Once the tea had been served Agnes asked her most pressing question.

"Have you come with news, Ella?"

I took a sip of my tea, giving me time to gather my thoughts. I needed to be careful for if it was proved Father Michael was murdered then Agnes would obviously become a suspect.

"Actually the lack of news is the reason I have come, Agnes."

"I'm sorry, I don't quite understand."

"I'll explain in a moment, but first I need to talk to you.

At present there is nothing to suggest the father's death was anything other than natural..."

"But..."

"I'm not saying it was, Agnes, and as it stands currently we have no evidence, but if proof were found that it was murder then my role will become official. Consequently our relationship will change. This goes for the other members of the church whom I know also. Do you understand?"

"But of course. You will be investigating on behalf of Scotland Yard. Therefore myself, Jocasta, and the others will automatically become suspects. But I knew this, Ella, and it's how it should be. I have nothing to hide and nor do the others. I trust you to do your job and find the culprit if there is one but it won't change my regard for you, nor our friendship. We just want to find out what happened, Ella, and we know you can help us do that."

"And you understand that if this becomes an official inquiry I will not be able to share any findings with you?"

"I do. Now is there anything I can do to help?"

"As a matter of fact there is. I need to get in contact with the Archbishop of York and thought you would be the best person to ask how it would be possible."

I briefly explained the delays Baxter had informed me of, the fact that direct liaison with the Church was in the hands of the Superintendent rather than us, and the hope that the Archbishop, as both a friend of the deceased and a man of notable position, could perhaps apply a little pressure in the right quarters. I might get in trouble by circumventing the normal protocol, but Baxter and I couldn't wait. We needed to know as soon as possible if this were a case of murder.

"I'm sure he can, in fact I'm positive of it. Daddy always said he was a man to be reckoned with once he had a bee in his bonnet about something, and this is much more important."

"Your father knew him?"

"Of course, Daddy was the Priest at St. Mary's before Father Michael took over. He and my mother married before he took his vows. Sorry I thought I'd mentioned it."

"No, you didn't. Does that mean you know the Archbishop?"

"Yes. Would you like me to telephone and explain the situation? I promise to be circumspect."

"Actually that's a very good idea, Agnes. I have no official capacity as yet, but as both a concerned parishioner and the daughter of the previous vicar, then it would only be natural for you to want to move things along. I believe a representative from Diocese is already on his way but according to Baxter, he didn't know Father Michael, so I doubt he'll be much help to us."

"I'll do it now. Would you like more tea while you wait?"

"Yes, all right, I would."

"I'll send Molly in."

Agnes returned just as Molly set down the new tea tray.

"Gosh, would you believe I just caught him in time, Ella, and he is going to make some calls. He would be here himself but is travelling to Rome tomorrow and won't be back for at least a week. Linhay doesn't fall under his jurisdiction as I'm sure you know, but he was a personal friend as well as Father Michael's spiritual adviser and is greatly perturbed at the delay. It's not only important that we find out what happened you see, but that Father Michael is laid to rest. His spirit is with his God now but his earthly remains need to be interred. There needs to be a funeral, Ella."

She took a handkerchief from her sleeve and dabbed her eyes beneath her glasses. The mention of a funeral had caused my heart to contract and an ice cold shiver to sweep from my head to my toes. The last funeral I had attended had been John's, and I remembered it with a clarity now as though it had been yesterday. I had to remind myself he was actually still alive, but the conversation with Agnes had left me with a terrifying feeling of foreboding.

"Sorry," she said, sniffing.

"There's no need to apologise, Agnes," I said softly, coming back to the present. "I realise this is a terrible ordeal for you and I promise we will do all we can to get a speedy resolution."

She nodded, and wiping her eyes a final time, tucked the handkerchief back into her sleeve.

"Thank you, Ella. There's to be a memorial service for Father Michael on Sunday, will you come?"

I promised I would do my best then took my leave. On the drive home I fervently hoped the Archbishop's telephone calls were yielding positive results.

The next morning sergeant Baxter telephoned bright and early with news.

"I don't know how you managed it, Miss Bridges, but I've just been told the post-mortem 'as been re-scheduled for this afternoon. With a bit of luck we should 'ave the cause of death confirmed by tomorrow at the latest."

"That is excellent news, Sergeant. Telephone as soon as you have the results."

Within four hours he called me back.

"My goodness that was quick," I said.

"I called to see the coroner on the off chance, you were right about it being murder. Father Michael was poisoned. I've squared it with the 'Top Brass,' we're now officially investigating."

"I knew it! What type of poison?"

"Ricin. Nasty stuff but common enough to get hold of if you know what yer doin'."

"Yes, from the beans of the Castor Oil plant, I believe. How was it administered do you know?"

"Let me look at me notes."

There was a rustle of paper as Baxter found the correct page.

"'Ere we are. 'A combination of ingestion and inhalation,' 'though he can't say how much of each."

"So it was in something he ate and breathed in?"

"So the coroner says. And not all at once neither, over

a short period of time apparently. He estimates exposure somewhere between three days to a week."

"Well, that may make our job more difficult, but it does suggest it was in something he had regular access to. Did the coroner tell you anything of the symptoms of this type of poison?" I asked.

"He did, and a bit too accurate if you ask me. I was in danger of losing me lunch several times. But I'll make it less grisly for you. Your question about how it were carried out were a good one as symptoms vary according to if it were breathed in, eaten or a needle were used. I'll stick with eaten or breathed in as it's what we know to be fact."

Sergeant Baxter went on to explain early symptoms of inhalation included a fever and a cough. Which we knew was correct in the vicar's case. Excessive thirst was indicative of ingestion.

"According to Mrs Markham, he consumed several cups of tea while with her, so that would certainly fit," I said.

With the use of his notebook, Baxter then went on to describe a litany of symptoms which made my blood run cold. These included pain, inflammation, hemorrhage, severe nausea, skin irritation and tightening of the chest. Eventually it would lead to organ failure and death.

"What an appalling way to die. Father Michael must have suffered a great deal."

"It's a rum do and no mistake, Miss Bridges."

"Well, I think we should keep this information under our

hats, Baxter. The last thing his friends and colleagues need is to know of his suffering. Now, what we need to do is to ascertain Father Michael's exact movements in the week or so leading up to his death. How soon can you be here?"

"There's a few things to sort out 'ere so it won't be before this evenin'. Mrs Baxter, is still at Elsie's, so I'll stay there. I'll meet you at the vicarage first thing. Do you know who 'as the keys?"

"I'll ask, Agnes. Can you get the local constable to guard the place until the morning? It's now officially part of a crime."

"Consider it done. I'll see yer tomorrow."

I telephoned Agnes and informed her the death of Father Michael was indeed deliberate and it was now officially a murder inquiry. I made no mention of poison and cautioned her against telling anyone else what I'd told her. It was vitally important she remained quiet, we didn't know who was responsible and we didn't want to tip off the culprit. I told her I would need the keys to the vicarage, and she informed me she still had the spare set which had belonged to her father. I arranged for Mrs Shaw to collect them post-haste.

After ringing off, I went through to the small sitting room where my aunt had organised lunch.

"It seems you have a difficult case, Ella."

"You heard? I'm afraid it won't be as straightforward as I'd hoped. It seems the fete was the place the vicar finally succumbed to the poison, as opposed to where the crime was committed. Now comes the daunting task of verifying

Father Michael's movements prior to his death, as well as trying to ascertain who would want to harm him and why. Not to mention how he came to consume enough poison over a period of time to kill him. As murders go this one is near perfect."

"There is no such thing as a perfect crime in my opinion. A murderer will always be punished whether in this life or the next."

"Well, if it's in the next it won't help me or Sergeant Baxter one jot."

"I have every faith in you both, Ella. Now, how about I beat you at a final game of Mau mau? I daresay you will be too busy to play after today."

"Yes, all right. And you can tell me all you know about the Castor Oil plant and their poisonous beans while we play. It appears Father Michael was killed using Ricin."

Chapter SIX

THERE WAS NO SIGN of the new priest the Church had sent when I arrived at the vicarage the following morning, but knowing it was now a crime scene, arrangements had been made for him to lodge in the village. Sergeant Baxter was waiting for me however.

"Good morning, Baxter."

"Miss Bridges," He replied with a nod.

"Nothing to report overnight?"

"No, I sent the young constable 'ome as soon as I got 'ere, he were almost asleep on 'is feet. But he said all were quiet, if a little spooky what with the graves being over yonder."

"I can imagine, it must be very different in the middle of the night. Now I think the key is for the door to the side."

The vicarage was everything I'd expected. A single level dwelling built of stone, not as old as the church itself, but still quite ancient. The interior was well appointed but leaned

announced he was to go on a sabbatical and a temporary vicar would take over during the interim. He returned the day you helped with the flowers as you know."

"Is it normal for a priest to leave his position for so long after just arriving?"

"Well, not normal particularly, but it's not unheard of. I suppose it would depend on the reasons he needed to leave."

"What sort of reasons are typical?"

"Illness perhaps or a crisis of faith. Special work for the church maybe, I really couldn't say. None of us knew Father Michael particularly well; he hadn't been here long enough."

"So you wouldn't know if he had any enemies?" asked Baxter.

Agnes looked up at him, wide owlish eyes blinking behind her thick lenses.

"Enemies? No. But of course he must have had one, mustn't he?"

"What about 'is family, do you know anything of them?"

"He has no siblings and his parents are both deceased. I suppose there may be extended family but I know nothing of them."

"And do you know what his appointments were since he returned?" I asked.

"I don't, I'm afraid. He was rather remiss about keeping his appointment book up to date, preferred to keep it all in his head. He had a very good memory."

There was little more Agnes could tell us so I sent her home. Once she'd left, Baxter and I explored the various rooms. The appointment book had told us nothing more than we already knew; unfortunately none of the rooms threw up any useful clues either. No threatening letters, no list of enemies and no convenient bottle marked poison stashed at the back of a cupboard. I sighed and went to look out of the bedroom window. I could see the church from this vantage point just the other side of the lane, and once again I spied the old gent in tweeds. He seemed to be staring in my direction. I had no idea who he was or what he wanted, but considering he was hovering about, I wondered if he was connected to the murder in some way.

"Well, that's the last of the rooms bar the kitchen," Baxter said coming to join me.

"Did you find anything useful?"

"Not a thing. I think we might need a miracle."

"I'm holding out for divine intervention personally."

Baxter laughed. "Well, if ever there were a case more fitting, I don't know of it."

The kitchen was old fashioned and functional at best. A large range, newly blackened, stood in the chimney breast to the right, with an assortment of copper pans and kettles hanging above. A curtain below the large glazed stoneware sink revealed nothing more than a bucket and a few cleaning rags. The central table of well-scrubbed pine was empty, and this is where we stacked the contents of the cupboards.

"Oh," I exclaimed as I opened a cupboard and found a familiar green and gold box. "I know this tea, it's made and sold in the town where my aunt lives and is the best in the land according to her. I remember Jocasta mentioning Father

Michael ordered his tea in specially."

"Well, let's box it up with the other foodstuffs for the lab boys to take a butcher's at. If the vicar were being poisoned over a number o' days it makes sense for it to be somewhere in this lot."

"We'll remove the contents of the drinks cabinet in the office too. How are we to get it all to London?"

"I've arranged for one of the local bobbies to take it, the lab is expecting him with some test items. So where to next?"

"I think lunch is in order I can't possibly think on an empty stomach. Then I believe we pay a visit to Mrs Jocasta Blenkinsop."

"The woman from the flower stall?"

"Precisely, Baxter. Let's see if she knows anything about growing Castor Oil plants."

Jocasta had married into money, and a great deal of it if the house were any indication. A Georgian pile of red brick with a plethora of windows and chimneys. The discreet sign at the gate had read, 'Briarlea Stud and Riding School,' and as we proceeded up the gravel drive we glimpsed horses grazing in distant paddocks and others being put through their paces by experienced riders. On the horizon was a large stable block where a group of children were being helped to mount a row of patiently waiting miniature horses.

"How the other half lives, eh?" said Baxter.

As we pulled up at the house a rider broke away and galloped towards us. Jocasta dismounted with practiced ease and handed the reins off to a waiting groom.

"Ella, I saw the car coming up the drive, what a lovely surprise."

She then noticed my companion.

"Ah, an official visit then? Give me a moment to change, I'll have Maud take you through to the drawing room."

Maud was patiently waiting by the front steps and gave a quick curtsy.

"This way, sir, madam."

We followed through the grand pillared portico flanked by large topiary bushes, and entered a hall of gargantuan proportions, with a chequered tile floor and numerous giant vases of eastern origin. Maud escorted us through to a drawing room with stunning views over the surrounding countryside, and informed us tea would be served shortly.

Baxter and I had briefly discussed how we would handle the interview on the drive over; he would wait for a suitable opening in the conversation to elicit the invitation we needed, hopefully without it being too obvious.

Maud arrived with the tea tray moments before Jocasta returned, freshly scrubbed and attired and smelling faintly of Lily of the Valley.

"So you've come about Father Michael's murder I assume? I must admit I was shocked when I heard the news. As awful

"It's a beautiful display," said Baxter, jumping on the opening we had discussed previously. "I meant to get something from your stall at the fete the other day for my wife, unfortunately I never got a chance."

"I grow them all myself in the hothouse and the greenhouses. I'll show you around before you go if you like? I'm sure we can find something suitable for you to take to your wife."

"That's very kind of you, Mrs Blenkinsop, I'd like that. And it'll certainly earn me a few brownie points with the missus."

Nicely done, Sergeant Baxter.

Finishing the arrangement Jocasta once again took her seat.

"I would say Father Michael already had something on his mind when he took over at St Mary's. But he was definitely much more worried over the last weeks since his return. Whether or not it was the same problem I can't tell you, but it does rather point to something happening before he arrived here, doesn't it? Perhaps it was the reason he took a sabbatical? The Archbishop of York would be able to tell you more of course, he and Father Michael were friends."

"Unfortunately, the Archbishop is currently in Rome and out of contact, but we will speak with him when he returns. You've been very helpful, Jocasta, however I think that's all we need to know for the moment," I said, rising from my chair.

"Well, you know where I am if you need to speak with me further. Come along, I'll give you both a tour of the greenhouses."

As we walked through the garden I inquired after Jocasta's health.

"Oh, I'm as right as rain now, thank goodness. We're awash with tourists at the moment, I must have caught a dose of something from one of them."

"And Anne and Prudence?"

"Well on the road to recovery too by all accounts, although Prudence is still a little shaky. Here we are."

She opened a large gate and led us through into a beautiful walled garden.

"Do you know, I've recently discovered a walled garden like this at my cottage? I hope I can do it the same justice you have here, it's quite stunning," I said, gazing around the space with pleasure.

"Well, I'm happy to give you or your gardener any pointers when you have time, planting marigolds in with your tomatoes for example keeps the insects away."

"I'll certainly pass along the tip, however it may be some time before we're at the stage of planting, although I really don't know for sure. Tom, my gardener, has requested I leave the entire project in his hands as he wants it to be a surprise, and I'm quite happy to do so."

I gazed around Jocasta's garden with deep appreciation.

"You certainly 'ave a fine array of produce here," said Baxter.

"The majority of fresh food for the house comes from this garden. The central beds as you can see are for the vegetables and the fruit bushes. The ones along the perimeter walls I use to grow cut flowers, carnations and daffs and whatnot, then we have the larger trained trees, such as apples and pears along the walls. And over here we're even experimenting with hops, my head gardener rather likes the idea of producing his own beer. Of course the staff deal with all of that, this here is my domain."

We entered quite the largest glass house I had ever seen, filled with tables on which stood a vast array of exotic flowering plants.

The temperature outside was extremely warm but inside it rose further by several degrees, and immediately I felt a thin sheen of perspiration form on my face and neck as the humidity hit me.

Above us were various hanging baskets each with a profusion of dangling greenery, and as we moved through the space I saw several beds had been dug into the ground from which large ferns, huge palms and smaller cacti grew. Baxter caught my eye and with a flick of his hand indicated to the left. I glanced over and nodded briefly. It was a Castor Oil plant.

"It's like walking through another world," said Baxter, obviously enchanted with the place.

"Marvellous, isn't it?" said Jocasta, oblivious to our exchange. "I visited The Royal Botanical Gardens at Kew when I was younger and fell in love. I vowed there and then I would have my own version when I grew up, and this is the result."

We meandered along wooden walkways taking in the

beauty of the specimens for some time before we reached another door. Jocasta opened it, hurried us through then quickly closed it. We were standing in a small square room with glass walls and ceiling.

"This allows us to preserve the temperature in the main area," she explained.

She opened another door opposite the last, and we stepped into what obviously was a behind-the-scenes work area. Rows of long trestle tables, on which an assortment of terracotta pots stood waiting for a small seed or bulb, greeted us. Hessian sacks full of compost were stacked underneath, a couple of wheelbarrows and various tools were scattered throughout, and above it all rose an earthy smell which reminded me of walking through an autumnal woodland on a bed of wet leaves.

"Through here is where the real work is done. Seed collection, potting out, taking cuttings and whatnot. Almost everything you saw next door started out life as a small cutting or a seed in here," Jocasta informed us as she continued the tour.

I realised one section of the original Victorian walled garden must have been removed in order to accommodate this space, as the back wall of this greenhouse had access to an external working area, where I saw several compost heaps being forked over by a gardener in shirtsleeves and a long jute apron. Beyond were hedgerows over which views of the surrounding fields could be seen.

I spied the broken pane just as Jocasta gave a cry of dismay.

Turning quickly, I saw a scene of utter chaos. A large bank of drawers such as you would find in an apothecary shop, had been well and truly ransacked. Drawers flung onto the floor where their contents had scattered far and wide.

"My seeds!"

Jocasta Blenkinsop had been burgled.

I asked Jocasta to see if she could ascertain what had been stolen, but under no circumstances was she to touch anything. We'd need to bring in a specialist to see if he could find some fingerprints. I took Baxter to one side out of earshot.

"I think we both know what she'll find," I whispered.

"Yes, but we need to be certain. Whoever it were made a right old mess."

"A distraction to conceal what they were really after perhaps? I don't suppose it will do any good to ask who had access?"

"We can ask but I doubt it'll help. The pane was broken from the outside, glass is on the inside you see, 'ere. They just climbed in, pinched what they wanted, wrecked the place to maybe cause confusion like you say, and went out the same way. It can't 'ave taken long. There's no sign of footprints in or out and they could 'ave come from anywhere. It's surrounded by open countryside, albeit most of what you can see is the Blenkinsop's land, but somehow I doubt a charge of trespass would bother someone with murder on their mind. No, it would 'ave been easy to get up 'ere unseen at night then return the same way," Baxter said, making notes in his little black book.

"We need to confirm when anyone was last in here. If the Ricin used to poison Father Michael originated as a Castor Oil bean here, then it had to have been over a week ago. I do think it's the case though, I noticed a fine layer of dust on the plundered drawers."

"Well if yer right, it's likely any trail outside will 'ave long since disappeared. I'm afraid our thief's trail is stone cold, but I'll go and 'ave a chat with that gardener out there on the off chance he saw or 'eard something."

As Baxter left to go outside I returned to Jocasta, who was on hands and knees carefully picking up discarded seeds and putting them into paper envelopes. There were hundreds, if not thousands of seeds ranging from those no bigger than a pin head, to some as large as a kidney bean. It would take weeks to sort them out properly.

"Have you found anything missing?" I asked gently.

"Four types so far. These drawers were all full and there's barely any of the seeds on the floor. Shouldn't have been full of course, I should have potted them up long before now but I've not been in here for over a month as my time has been taken up elsewhere. Why on earth would someone break in to steal my seeds? All they had to do was ask and I'd have gladly given them some, and told them how to grow and look after them. It doesn't make sense. Damn it! It's going to take years for me to get the collection back up to what it was."

She pointed to the four drawers and I looked at the labels.

"These are in Latin? Not my strong point I'm afraid," I said.

"Of course, sorry. Look, do you mind if I sit, I'm losing all feeling in my legs?"

She rose and went to a nearby bench where she still had a close view of the drawers, then explained what they had contained.

"Now let's have a look. Ageratina altissima, that's white snakeroot, Ricinus communis is the Castor Oil plant. Nerium oleander is the oleander, and Abrus precatorius is the Rosary..."

She tailed off and looked at me with wide eyes.

"What is it?"

"Ella, every single one of these is poisonous."

I left Jocasta having elicited a promise from her not to tell anyone about what was missing, and also made a suggestion to keep the seeds under lock and key from now on. Rather a case of shutting the greenhouse door after the thief had already bolted, but there was nothing else for it. I went in search of Baxter. He'd just finished speaking with the gardener and walked over to join me.

"Well, the gardener, Archer's his name, didn't 'ear nor see

a thing. Not being able to pinpoint the time of the theft is a bit of a problem of course, but he's never even been inside the greenhouses. Only the head bloke, a man called..."

Here he consulted his black book.

"Peterson, and Mrs Blenkinsop 'erself ever worked with the exotic stuff. But Archer assures me Peterson hasn't set foot in the place for more'n a month, other duties apparently."

"I think we may have a bigger problem," I said, and proceeded to tell him what Jocasta had discovered.

"Well, that does shed a different light on things. We're obviously looking for someone with specialist knowledge if they could pick out poisonous seeds, not only from that lot but by their Latin names. And so far we only know of one person who fits that particular bill."

We both turned back to look at the greenhouse behind us, and to where Jocasta was back on her hands and knees amongst the scattered seeds.

"She certainly has both means and opportunity but what could her motive be? And why go to the trouble of making it look like a break in? Surely she must realise the evidence is pointing in her direction?" I said.

"Could be like you said earlier, causes confusion and throws the investigation in a different direction. But either she's innocent or 'as been far too clever for 'er own good. Our job now is to find out what 'er motive could be while also looking for other potential suspects."

"Nothing too complicated then," I said as we made our

way back to the greenhouse and asked to use the telephone.

Jocasta accompanied us back the way we'd come, having thrust a delicate looking orchid in Baxter's arms as we'd left the greenhouse.

"I thought you might like to take this for your wife. Keep it indoors in a light warm spot, kitchen would be best as it likes a little humidity, but be careful not to over water it."

"Well that's very kind, Mrs Blenkinsop, I'm sure Mrs Baxter will cherish it. How much do I owe yer."

"Consider it a gift, Sergeant."

"I'm afraid I can't do that, not while on the job yer understand. Plus it's for a good cause, the new meeting room at St Mary's?"

"Well, if you insist. Thank you."

Back at the house she took Baxter to the telephone. He called The Yard and ordered a team to search the scene of the crime for fingerprints, then contacted a local bobby to guard it while they arrived. We then returned to the greenhouse to wait. It wasn't long before the constable arrived and once Baxter had explained the situation we returned to the car.

"Do you think she was trying to bribe you with an orchid?" I asked him.

We were making our way to the guest house where Mrs Baxter was getting ready to accompany her husband back to London. He intended to go to the police laboratory first thing next morning to see if he could chivvy along the tests on the food from the vicarage. We needed to confirm the source of the poison and the vicarage foodstuff was our only clue at this stage.

"I doubt it, but it's best not to muddy the waters."

"I've been thinking. Two points concern me at the moment."

"Only two?" said Baxter wryly.

"The first is we only have Jocasta's word for the fact the seeds are missing. And the second, if they have been stolen, then perhaps Father Michael isn't the only victim. Maybe he was a test of sorts and the thief is planning on using the other seeds on someone else? It could be the vicar wasn't the intended target at all but was in fact killed in order to throw our suspicion that way, guaranteeing our time will be taken up investigating while one or more murders take place elsewhere."

Baxter turned and stared at me, a look of horror on his face.

"What a terrifyin' thought! And 'ere I was worrying about muddying the waters by accepting a plant. I admit it's not an impossible idea, although it's not far off. But we can't investigate 'what ifs' and 'maybes.' No we 'ave to stick to the facts as we know 'em, gather evidence and move the case forward. All things bein' equal we'll find our murderer. But if the evidence points us in more than one direction then we'll just 'ave to follow it. You have an uncanny knack for this type of work, Miss Bridges, and yer mind works in astonishing ways, but I 'ope for all our sakes yer wrong about this."

I dropped him off at the guest-house with a reminder of the memorial service for Father Michael.

"Do you think it would be prudent to go?" I asked.

ebratory wake, shared stories of the deceased, music, dancing plus lots of alcohol of course. Although I concede the weather today is well suited for the occasion. Shall we go in?"

"We may as well, the last of the stragglers are makin' their way in now, it looks as though the entire village 'as turned up, we'll be 'ard pressed to get a pew. No matter, we'll 'ave a better vantage point if we're stood at the back."

Baxter was right, the church was packed tight and it was standing room only. We squashed in at the rear not far from the door where we had a good view, but although I recognised a few faces, in the main they were unknown to me. Baxter not being a resident was faced with a sea of strangers apart from those he'd met during the investigation, and I was beginning to think this was a foolhardy quest.

Just over an hour later, having listened to Father Michael's replacement, the ancient Father Jacob, speak in both English and Latin, interspersed with several hymns and a few bouts of sobbing, it was over, and we quickly moved outside. Thank goodness the rain had stopped. I was jostled several times and Baxter took my elbow to prevent me from falling. I was trying to move unsuccessfully out of the way when I was bumped into quite roughly, luckily Baxter was once again on hand otherwise I would have found myself face down on the path.

"Sorry Miss," a young girl said as she charged down the path.

I caught nothing more than a pale face covered in freckles and wisps of red hair under a hat, before a hand was laid on my arm and I turned to its owner. It was Agnes.

"Thank you for coming, Ella."

"It was a lovely service and very well patronised," I told her.

"Yes, although he hadn't been here very long, Father Michael was well liked, particularly by the elder parishioners as he visited them quite often. He will be missed by everyone."

I looked around for Baxter whom I seemed to have lost in the crowd, and eventually spied him leaning against the wall not far from the gate. He raised a hand.

"Listen, Agnes, I'm afraid I must go. Will you be all right?"

"Yes, of course I will. I need to go and find mother anyway, I left her with Jocasta. Goodbye, Ella."

"I can't say I learned much at all from that exercise. What about you?" I asked Baxter as I drove him back to the train station.

"Not much at all I'm afraid, although it'll have done our image no 'arm to 'ave been seen."

"Do you think the murderer was there?"

"Hard to say. Possibly, but there were certainly nothing obvious."

"When do you think the lab will have some results for us?"

"Not fer a couple of days yet I shouldn't think, but I'll let you know as soon as I 'ear anything."

I said goodbye to Baxter and drove back to the cottage. With a few days grace before we could do anything more I vowed to spend a bit more time on the compendium and with my aunt, who I felt quite guilty at leaving to her own devices considering she was my guest.

in silence. My aunt and I sat in the back and she gripped my hand the entire time. I was grateful for the contact and the comfort it brought, I'd never felt so alone.

After what seemed like hours we pulled up at a barrier where a guard spoke to Mrs Shaw through the window, peered into the back at us, then saluted. Moving the barrier to one side he stood in position saluting while we drove forward. Five minutes later we were pulling up outside a hangar where an official-looking black car was waiting and a familiar figure alighted.

"Miss Bridges," said the Home Secretary. "Please accept my sincere condolences. I'm terribly sorry for your loss."

Dusk was almost upon us and a dark looming sky threatened rain overhead. Baxter was right, it was fitting.

"What can you tell me?" I asked.

"We received notification that an aircraft of German make had crashed in a farmer's field in Scotland. There were three men aboard, the pilot and two passengers. Both the pilot and one of the passengers have yet to be formally identified but we believe them to be German. The other passenger was your husband. We had no prior intelligence to indicate this aircraft was headed here, nor the reasons why."

"But you believe John was aiding a member of the German government who wished to escape?"

"It's a theory but that's all it is, we have no way of knowing. However we are looking into it. I'm afraid that's all I can tell you, Miss Bridges."

I nodded.

"I'd like to see my husband now, Lord Carrick," I said in a voice I didn't recognise.

The hangar was a cavernous space, cold and mostly empty but all I saw was a casket on a table in the centre, lid raised waiting for me to lay eyes on my husband for the last time. I took a deep breath and clutching Aunt Margaret's arm I walked forward on legs that felt as weak as a new born colt's.

I spent the next two days in bed, listless, lethargic and utterly exhausted having cried a well of tears. I had recognised John straightaway, although he had changed considerably since the last time I had seen him. There was a smattering of grey in his hair, fine lines at his eyes and mouth and he'd lost weight, the stresses and strains of his job I supposed. But in the main he was the husband I had once known and loved, and now I had lost him forever.

I turned as the door opened and Aunt Margaret came in bearing a breakfast tray. She had done the same thing each morning since we'd returned and had taken it away again a few hours later, barely touched. This time she laid the tray as normal but then sat on my bed.

"Ella, you can't go on like this, it's doing you no good at all. You need to get up today. Sergeant Baxter has called and so has Agnes, and I've made your excuses but I shan't do it anymore, you need to speak with them yourself. Now I'm not leaving until you've eaten every last crumb of your breakfast, you need to keep your energy up."

And so she went on, badgering, cajoling and bullying until I sat up and began to nibble at the toast.

"It's not much fun being here alone, you know. Of course I'm quite capable of keeping myself occupied but it's difficult when it's not one's own house."

"Not above a little blackmail, I see?"

"Anything to get you to join the living again, dear. Did it work?"

"Yes, of course it did," I said with a brief smile.

"I'm glad, Ella, we are all missing you downstairs."

"Do you know, Aunt Margaret, I must be the only woman ever to have been widowed twice by the same man."

"Perhaps not the only one, darling, but undoubtedly it's a very exclusive club. Now finish your tea and I'll take your tray."

Half an hour later I was dressed and made my way downstairs feeling more human than I had for a while. The message from Baxter was simply that there was no news from the food tests as yet, but he would let me know as soon as he heard. The one from Agnes said she'd be grateful if I could accompany her to visit Mrs Whittingstall, if my time allowed.

"It will do you good to get out, Ella, and with the case at a standstill you have time on your hands. From what I understand from Agnes, the woman might appreciate some female company, her husband is quite ill."

"Would you like to come, Aunt Margaret?"

"I'm afraid I can't. I met an old friend, Constance Burridge, on the promenade yesterday and we're meeting for tea and canasta later."

"Burridge? Of Burridge's department store?" I asked.

"That's the one. She's here with her sister. Sir Algernon is far too busy running the empire to accompany her."

"I didn't realise you knew Lady Burridge, how did the two of you meet?"

"Oh, I met her husband first. I helped him out of a rather sticky situation regarding a set of counterfeit Ming vases and a high stakes poker game. Constance and I became firm friends after that. Now if there's nothing else, dear, I need to get on." And she departed the drawing room like a ship in full sail.

"Would you like me to drive you to the hotel?" I called to her retreating back.

"No need, darling, Constance is sending a car."

I'd arranged to pick Agnes up at St. Mary's and as I parked she came hurrying out from under the lych-gate, a basket covered in a red and white checked cloth over her arm.

"Hello, Ella," she said breathlessly. "Thank you for coming with me. I do hope you are feeling better now, your aunt said you've been feeling a bit below par?"

"I'm quite well now, Agnes, thank you for asking."

"Is there any news about the investigation?" she whispered,

even though there was only the two of us in the car.

"Nothing as yet, inquiries are still ongoing. There's some delicious smells coming from that basket. Is it a gift for Mrs Whittingstall?"

"Yes, mother and I have baked some scones and an apple pie for her, I doubt she has much time to bake, what with nursing her husband."

"She doesn't have a cook?"

"As far as I know it's just the two of them. She prefers it that way I suppose as they aren't short of money for help."

"What time is she expecting us?"

"Um, actually I'm afraid she isn't. Sorry, I had no way of contacting her you see, only directions to the house. Oh dear, do you think it will be all right?"

Taking my eyes off the road for a moment I glanced at her. Her large eyes were filled with worry and an embarrassed hue tinged her cheeks.

"Well, either we will be made welcome or it will be a short-lived visit, either way our intentions are good. But we'll soon find out. I believe this is the place?"

Agnes peered through the windscreen.

"Yes, this is it."

I parked the car outside and we walked up the short drive to the front door. The house was quite large with a small garden to the front laid mostly to lawn, and a few wilted shrubs striving for life on its periphery. From the road the house had looked quite well kept but close to it was apparent it needed work. The paint was beginning to peel from the front door and several of the window frames were rotten. The glass panes themselves were quite clean but behind them were net curtains so thick it was impossible to see inside.

Agnes knocked on the door and almost immediately I saw a slight twitch of a curtain in the right hand side window. But several seconds passed and no one answered, so I knocked again a little louder. This time someone came.

I didn't know what I'd expected but the stunning young woman before us was certainly not it. She was quite beautiful with a flawless complexion, light blue eyes and a discreet beauty mark above the right side of her lip. Her pale blond hair was perfectly set in waves and curled about petite ears, which in turn were set with small diamond and pearl earrings. She looked familiar but I couldn't think where I'd seen her before unless it was at the church. Yes, of course, this was the lady who had knocked into me that first day. With everything that had happened since I'd forgotten all about it.

"Can I help you?" she asked in perfectly modulated tones.

"Mrs Whittingstall?" asked Agnes quietly.

"Yes."

"My name is Agnes, and this is my friend Ella. We're from the 'Friends of St. Mary's.'"

"If you're looking for a donation I'm afraid..."

"Oh, goodness me, no, nothing of the sort. Sorry, we just came to visit to see if there is anything we could do for you. My mother and I..."

While Agnes explained our impromptu visit to the perplexed Mrs Whittingstall I took in what little I could see of the house behind her. Next to the door was an oak hall stand filled with several umbrellas, walking canes, three golf clubs and disconcertingly, a shotgun. The latter of which I fervently hoped wasn't loaded as our visit hadn't been particularly well received. Above were several hooks on which hung a variety of outdoor coats and hats. Beyond was a small sideboard with a framed photograph, which I could barely make out but thought was of an older gentleman dressed in shooting clothes, a shotgun over his shoulder, proudly holding up a brace of pheasants. On the far wall facing the door was a painting by an artist I was familiar with and when Agnes paused for breath I mentioned it.

"I see you have a DuPont, Mrs Whittingstall. I've recently acquired one myself."

"I beg your pardon?"

"The painting on your wall back there, a Pierre DuPont?"

She glanced behind her then shrugged elegantly.

"It's my husband's. I know nothing of it. Now if there is nothing else..."

"Just the apple pie and scones," said Agnes raising her basket with a smile.

"I'm afraid I don't like apple pie, or scones, and my husband is unable to eat them. In fact, I believe I've just heard his bell. If you'll excuse me..."

And with that she shut the door.

Agnes and I looked at each other in mutual shock at her rudeness.

"Oh dear," she sniffed, the sparkling of unshed tears in her eyes.

"Don't let her upset you, Agnes, not everyone is as gracious or generous as you. Come on, I think afternoon tea is in order, and I believe there is a lovely little tea shop on the promenade which has just opened."

We were halfway down the drive when we were met by the postman who was delivering a letter.

"Good afternoon, Miss Bridges, Miss Shepherd," he said, tipping his hat. "A lovely day for a visit, isn't it?"

"It is a lovely day although it was rather a short visit. I'm afraid I should have called ahead, we caught her unexpectedly," said Agnes dejectedly.

"Oh, I wouldn't worry too much, Miss Shepherd, she's a bit of a strange one, very private. Well, I'll not keep you. You have a good afternoon."

We said our goodbyes and carried on to the car, but not before I had seen the return address of the letter he was delivering, nor the black cat with purple collar sitting on the garden wall, eying the house with haughty disdain. It appeared as though Phantom didn't like Mrs Whittingstall much either.

Chapter EIGHT

I RETURNED HOME IN THE EARLY EVENING having had a lovely afternoon with Agnes. She had cheered up enormously and insisted I take the pie and scones home.

"It would be such a shame to waste them and we already have far more than we can eat ourselves," she said.

So of course I acquiesced, the tempting smells had been making my mouth water all afternoon.

I found Mrs Shaw in my office, working on the compendium, but of Aunt Margaret there was no sign.

"Has my aunt not returned yet?"

"She telephoned earlier to say she would be staying on for dinner and not to wait up. She sounded in high spirits."

I smiled to myself. Knowing my aunt as I was beginning to, I wouldn't be surprised if the sedate game of canasta had turned into a rousing game of poker, to which half the hotel had been invited.

"Oh, and this came for you. Special delivery."

Mrs Shaw handed me a large cardboard folder. Quickly untying the red ribbon I carefully opened it and removed the handwritten note. It was from Sergeant Baxter.

"Mrs Shaw, come and look at these."

"My goodness, they're wonderful and perfect for the compendium. He certainly is a man of many talents," she said as she peered over my shoulder at the exquisitely rendered drawings.

"He is indeed. He's as good a detective as he is an artist too. His note says he's been spending some time in various parts of London, drawing from life."

"Well, he's certainly captured a broad representation of people, that's for sure. From the wealthy having a constitutional around Hyde Park, to the poor of the East End and everything in between it looks like."

"Criminals come in all shapes and sizes and from all walks of life as Sergeant Baxter well knows. I think he's done an exceptional job and I shall call to tell him so in the morning."

But as it happened I didn't get the chance, for he telephoned me first thing the next day with the news we had been waiting for.

"I received the results from the laboratory this morning. We were right, Miss Bridges."

"Where was it found?" I asked.

"I don't want to say more over the telephone, but I'm booked on the next train and will be at Linhay station at ten thirty."

"I'll have Mrs Shaw meet you and bring you back to the

"Yes, Carnaby's Emporium. It's in a small town called Broughton not far from Sheffield. It's where Aunt Margaret lives actually. I visited the emporium last time I was there."

"How is yer aunt by the way? Is she still with you, I didn't see 'er this mornin'?"

"Oh yes, she's still here but she was up and out early. She has some friends staying at the hotel and had made arrangements to spend the day with them. Baxter, do you think it's possible the poison was introduced into the tea at Carnaby's before it was delivered to the vicarage?"

"I find anythin' is possible when it comes to murder, Miss Bridges, it's staggerin' the lengths some people will go to. We'll keep it at the back of our minds but I think the best course is to follow up clues nearer to 'ome first, rather than tearin' all over the country."

"Yes, I suppose it's not the best use of our time. Nonetheless, if it's all right with you I think I will speak to Aunt Margaret and see what she can find out. She's one of their best customers and I suspect she knows the owner."

"It can't do any harm, and the more we know the better; we'll be prepared should a visit be required."

"My thoughts exactly. Now I think I'll drive around to the servants' entrance," I said as we reached the turning for the Blenkinsop's house and started up the drive.

"Catch 'em unprepared," Baxter nodded approvingly.

"You never know what we may find."

I parked the car a reasonable distance from the door so as

not to announce our arrival too soon, and just as I had switched off the engine a pale young girl with freckles and tendrils of red hair escaping from her cap came out into the yard carrying a bucket overflowing with dirty water.

"That's her. She must be the scullery maid," I said.

"We're on the right track then, Miss Bridges. Let's make the acquaintance of the 'ousekeeper then we can ask to speak to this maid. What were the 'ousekeeper's name again?"

"Mrs Brown."

By the time we reached the door to the kitchen the maid had disappeared, but we were greeted by a footman named Johnson who had been taking a quick break to smoke a cigarette around the corner.

"Here to see Mrs Brown, you say? I'll take you to her office if you'd like to follow me," he said amiably.

We followed him through the busy kitchen and down a long hallway, where open doors showed a range of servants hard at work polishing boots, ironing laundry, mending clothes, cleaning silver and a vast array of other duties needed to keep a large household running smoothly. Presently we came to an unremarkable door, where the footman knocked once and upon hearing a reply opened it.

"Visitors, Mrs Brown. A Miss Bridges and a Sergeant Baxter."

"Of course, do come in and have a seat. Johnson, go and ask Tilly to prepare a tea tray please."

Once Johnson had left in search of Tilly, Mrs Brown turned back to us. She was a neat woman of middling height

Mrs Brown paused here for a moment as though trying to think of a suitably tactful reply.

"To be honest, we all thought it was a bit strange when he left, but you can't know what goes through a young man's mind, can you? According to Mrs Blenkinsop, he had found a better position elsewhere."

"She came and told you that herself, did she?" I asked.

"Yes. Gathered us all in the kitchen yonder and announced that he had left the previous evening. We didn't see him again."

"When were this?" Baxter asked, still furiously scribbling.

"Toward the end of September. But how does this have anything to do with the death of the vicar?"

Baxter smiled genially.

"We're not sure it does, Mrs Brown, just getting the facts straight is all. Can you tell us if Father Michael ever visited 'ere?"

"I believe he came to see Mrs Blenkinsop two or three times when he first arrived, although he did have a tendency to turn up unannounced on that bicycle of his so it could have been more. Church business I supposed, she's heavily involved with the fundraising and does the flowers, you see. Although I hadn't seen him for a long time before... well before he passed on."

"Thank you, Mrs Brown," I said. "I think that's all for the moment. Now we'd like to have a word with Betty, in private. Would you like us to use another room or can we remain in here? I don't want to put you out of your office if it's inconvenient."

"Oh, er, of course you can stay in here. I need to speak

with the cook about tomorrow's menu anyway. But are you sure it's Betty, you wish to speak to? She's just a simple scullery maid, I doubt she knows anything of use."

"Quite sure, Mrs Brown, thank you."

"All right, well, I'll send her in and find out what's keeping Tilly with the tea."

Tilly came in not long after Mrs Brown had left and laid the tea tray in silence. Giving a small curtsy she left as quietly as she had arrived, and Baxter and I were left alone while we waited for Betty.

"So what are yer thoughts so far, Miss Bridges?"

"I think after we have spoken to Betty, we need to find the groom Dawkins. There is most assuredly more going on in that regard than at first appears."

"They're my thoughts too. I 'ave a nasty feeling we're about to find out something that'll blow this case wide open."

I sighed heavily. "A possible motive you mean?"

Baxter nodded.

I began to pour the tea, my mind in a whirl, when the door suddenly opened and Betty entered. She was even younger than I had first thought, thirteen or fourteen perhaps, certainly no older.

"Sit down, Betty," I said without preamble, indicating Mrs Brown's recently vacated chair. She hesitated for a moment,

then did as she was told. "I'll come straight to the point."
Reaching into my bag I removed the note and laid it on the
desk in front of her. "You slipped this into my pocket at Father
Michael's memorial service the other day. Why?"

"Twern't me, miss."

I had been prepared for such a denial after the description
of the girl from Mrs Brown.

"It seems you haven't been as clever as you think you have,
Betty. You see I recognise you. Bumping into me as harshly
as you did nearly made me fall so I was bound to look to see
who was responsible. Plus of course, Sergeant Baxter and myself
are detectives, very good ones in fact, and I'm sure the fingerprints on this note will undoubtedly match yours. Did you
know fingerprints can be taken from notes such as this and
matched to a specific person? No two prints are the same, you
see. I learned that in my previous murder case. A case which I
solved by the way. Now do you want to try again? What does
this note mean and why did you put it in my pocket?"

At my deliberately stern pronouncement Betty's plain
plump face crumpled and she dissolved into floods of tears. I
fished in my bag for a handkerchief, which she filled noisily
then tried to return.

"Do keep it," I said.

"She took 'im from me. He loved me and she took 'im
from me," she suddenly blurted out.

"Who do you mean, Betty? Mrs Blenkinsop?"

She nodded.

"Who did she take from you?"

"Alfie," she wailed amid another bout of tears.

I looked at Baxter who shrugged and nodded for me to continue. Obviously dealing with hysterical young girls was to be my job.

"Do you mean Alfred Dawkins, the groom?"

She nodded again and looked up at me. Her pale skin had broken out into ugly red blotches and her eyes were swollen from all the tears. She looked positively wretched.

"Look, just tell us exactly what happened, Betty, from the beginning."

"I saw 'em together. T'were me afternoon off and I was just comin' round the corner of the 'ouse when I saw the vicar leavin' the stables. He looked like he'd seen a ghost, so I sneaked round the side and that's when I saw 'em. They was undressed and had been lyin' in the hay. The mistress grabbed a blanket and ran to the stable door. She must 'ave seen the vicar cyclin' away 'cos she came back and said to Alfie to get dressed quickly and leave, and to keep 'is mouth shut. Next day he was gone."

I glanced at Baxter's notebook while Betty recovered herself and saw him underline the word motive twice.

We'd eventually extracted information from Betty which led us to believe Alfred Dawkins was currently employed at the Hardcastle Livery Stables, situated on the northern side of Linhay. So we said our goodbyes and with an air of gloom set off to find him.

"It all fits," said Baxter a while later.

"I know."

"Once we've got this Dawkins's statement we'll 'ave to formally interview Mrs Blenkinsop."

"Yes. She's back from London early tomorrow evening. I suppose we'll have to do it then?"

"We'll 'ave to make sure we're there when she arrives, no doubt 'er staff will mention our visit if they get to 'er first. I only 'ope Betty keeps quiet like she promised."

"I'm quite sure she will, Baxter. Don't forget she saw Jocasta and this Dawkins in the stable herself, yet she hasn't mentioned it to anyone. The only time she has broken her silence was when she found out Father Michael was dead and she made contact with me via the note. Even then she tried to do it anonymously."

"Well I 'ope you're right."

"Jocasta is coming in on the quarter to five train by the way, perhaps we could contrive to be at the station to meet her? By coincidence naturally. Of course we'll have to let her driver know not to pick her up."

"Leave it with me," he said, and we once more lapsed into silence, each of us with our own thoughts.

The more we'd talked to Betty the more pity I had felt for her. She'd been brought up by a drunk and absentee father, who had finally met his maker by way of two bottles of cheap whiskey and the river two years ago, her mother having passed on when she was just six. The Friends of St Mary's had taken it upon themselves to find her gainful employment to avoid the orphanage, or worse, a Public Assistance Institution. Which up until five years ago was aptly named The Workhouse. Jocasta had stepped forward with a position of scullery maid and Betty had been in her employ ever since.

However, I was having difficulty uniting this plain simple girl with the description Mrs Brown had given us of 'the exceptionally handsome' Alfie Dawkins, and so had asked...

"Betty, did you and Alfie have an understanding?"

At her look of incomprehension I tried again.

"I mean to say did you think that you and Alfie were a couple?"

She looked up at me coyly through swollen red-rimmed eyes, and short lashes so pale they were almost invisible and said...

"I think so, miss."

"And what made you think so, Betty?"

"He were nice to me, miss. He talked to me when he come up to the 'ouse, and he brought me a posy once, daisies and the like from the back field."

"I see. And did he talk to the other girls or bring them posies?" I asked gently.

She shrugged, a sullen look on her face.

"S'pose so. But mine were nicer and he talked to me more."

I'd left it then, no longer wishing to pry into the heart

of a young and impressionable girl, who had been so devoid of love and affection for most of her life that she'd latched onto the first person who showed her any true kindness.

Baxter's voice when he suddenly spoke made me jump, as I'd been completely lost in my thoughts.

"We're here, Miss Bridges."

The Hardcastle Livery Stables was a very well patronised and thriving business, catering to the rich and famous who paid a weekly fee for their horses to be taken care of, and who occasionally visited when a suitable gap in their social calendar allowed. It was run in the main by a manager, the owner being a foreign gentleman who rarely set foot in the country, and he came out of the office to greet us as we pulled up.

"Good afternoon, may I help you?"

Baxter introduced us both and explained why we were there.

"Alfie Dawkins? Yes, you'll find him over in the stable block. Not in any trouble, is he? I don't employ troublemakers here."

"No trouble, we just 'ave some questions regarding 'is previous employer."

"All right, well just go through the archway there and follow the path round to the right. The stable block's at the end."

We thanked the manager and proceeded to the afore-mentioned block, where we found an athletically built youth in shirtsleeves grooming a beautiful bay mare. There was no doubt this was Alfie Dawkins, Mrs Brown's description had been highly accurate. He was perhaps twenty years of age, six feet tall, with jet black hair styled slightly longer than was fashionable, and which flopped over his forehead momentarily hiding deep brown eyes. Kind eyes, filled with humour and intelligence. He flashed a friendly smile on our approach, displaying a set of perfectly straight white teeth. This was a young man who was completely at ease with himself. A modern-day Adonis who would have caused the heart of the most stoical old maid to flutter, but I believed he truly had no idea how breathtaking he was.

"Alfie Dawkins?" inquired Baxter.

"Yes, Sir?"

"Sergeant Baxter, and this 'ere is Miss Bridges. We'd like to ask you a few questions about Mrs Blenkinsop. I understand you were employed by her previously?"

"That's right I was. Is she all right, Sergeant?"

The concern on his face was genuine and I saw immediately he had cared for Jocasta a great deal.

"For the moment she is, son. Can you tell me the circumstances which led to your dismissal from Briarlea?"

"I'm sure you know the circumstances, Sergeant, otherwise you wouldn't be here. But I wasn't dismissed. I chose to go."

"You did, did you? And why was that? You 'ad a good job there, a regular wage and plenty of scope for promotion. Why give it all up voluntarily? What made you do it?"

"To save the reputation of a woman you'd come to care for. That's right, isn't it?" I said to the youth.

"I see. A high level managerial position with considerable responsibility. How does he feel about you working as a groom? You mentioned he was rather put out at your securing the job at Briarlea."

"I suppose it's natural for all fathers to want their sons to follow in their footsteps, and mine was no different. But from the moment I could walk I've been happiest outdoors among the animals and nature. Mother thinks I was born with the soul of a nomad or a gypsy and I think she's right. My father was somewhat disappointed initially, but even he could see how miserable I would have been if he'd forced me. He's come round now and is perfectly accepting of my working with horses. Especially considering my younger sister Emily is showing signs of being very interested in engineering."

"Do you attend church?" asked Baxter.

If Alfie was surprised at the abrupt change in subject he didn't show it. Instead he spread his arms wide.

"This is my church, Sergeant Baxter. We're all God's creations, are we not? From the lowliest beetle to the King of the land. I don't need a building to worship in to be a good Christian. Many people do and that's their way, it's just not mine."

It struck me then how much Aunt Margaret and this young man had in common, and if circumstances had been different I'm sure they could have found themselves in an odd sort of friendship.

It was a second or two later as Baxter and I kept walking

that we realised Alfie had stopped, so we turned around. He eyed us thoughtfully for a moment then spoke.

"Well, I'm certainly slow on the uptake today. You're here about the death of the vicar, aren't you?"

He indicated we should make the return journey to the stables, so we continued to walk back the way we'd come.

"Yes, we are. Did you know Father Michael?" Baxter asked.

"Never had the pleasure."

"We 'ave been led to believe the day afore you left Briarlea for good, Father Michael chanced upon you and Mrs Blenkinsop together in the stables. Can you shed any further light on that, son?"

"Not really, I didn't see him myself. Jocasta said she heard a noise so she grabbed a horse blanket and went to the stable door. She returned saying she'd just seen the vicar bicycling down the drive and she was convinced he'd seen us. We parted ways, but that night she sought me out in floods of tears, terrified her husband would find out. I calmed her down and explained that for her sake it would be best if I left. She disagreed to start with, but we talked it through and eventually she came to realise it was the only option. I haven't seen her since."

"Do you know..." he continued as we neared the stables.

"One of the jobs we have is to get rid of the mice and rats? They come in for the horse feed and make their little nests in the hay, if you don't do something about them you're quite overrun in a matter of weeks. It was the same up at Briarlea, but instead of putting down poison Jocasta made these little traps that would catch them unharmed, ingenious little device actually. Then she'd drive up to the woods or down to the river and set them free. She said they were God's creatures as much as we were and what right did we have to kill them?"

He stopped as we approached the stable bay where he'd returned the mare earlier, and looked at us both in turn.

"If you think Jocasta had anything to do with the death of Father Michael, you're wrong. Someone who couldn't even bring themselves to kill a rat could never hurt another human being."

Chapter NINE

IT WAS EARLY EVENING by the time I returned to the cottage after dropping Baxter off at Elsie's boarding house, and I was absolutely famished. I'd had nothing to eat since the mid-morning tea and my stomach was literally growling in complaint.

I found Aunt Margaret in the small sitting room waiting for me.

"Ella, there you are, dear. Did you have a successful day?" she asked, laying the book she had been reading on the side table.

I flopped down in a chair suddenly exhausted.

"Well we certainly know a lot more now than we did, Aunt. I'll explain everything shortly, but I must eat first, I'm feeling quite faint with hunger."

"Yes, I thought that might be the case, dinner will be ready in ten minutes so you just have time to change."

I scurried upstairs and came down ten minutes later to the sounds of clinking crockery coming from the dining room.

"Salmon-en-Croute, new potatoes in herb butter and a medley of vegetables," my aunt announced, lifting various lids.

"My goodness, did Mrs Parsons make all this?"

"Of course not, dear, I had it delivered from the hotel. I fancied something a little different and the chefs there are quite excellent. There's treacle tart for desert."

"Oh, Aunt Margaret, I feel quite ashamed. I've been neglecting you terribly, haven't I?"

"Absolute nonsense, I'm having a perfectly lovely time. However, please promise me that when this case is over you will make a concerted effort to find yourself some proper staff? You need a full-time cook, a housekeeper and a maid, you're becoming far too busy to manage everything alone and Mrs Shaw will be leaving soon."

"Oh dear, yes I suppose she will be now John has been found and the news leaked to those that were a threat. I hadn't given it much thought to be honest, she's become rather a fixture around the place."

I ate with unseemly gusto as I mused on how to broach a particular subject with Mrs Shaw. It had been on my mind since I'd found out her true purpose for being here, but I'd come up blank as to the best way to ask, it was such an unseemly subject.

"I know what you're thinking," my aunt said.

I laughed out loud at the pronouncement knowing full well she probably did.

"Do tell."

"Mrs Shaw's wages. You were paying her as your house-keeper before you knew who she really was, but she was also being paid by the Home Office."

I stared open-mouthed.

"How do you do that?"

"It's a gift, dear."

"You'd make a lot of money as a fortune teller you know."

"It's uncanny you should say that... but no, that's another story. Rest assured it's all been quite above board, the wages you paid have all been deposited back into your bank account and Mrs Shaw has all the necessary receipts."

"Well, that is a relief, I was worrying about how to raise the subject. Thank you, Aunt Margaret."

"Think nothing of it, Ella. Now tell me where have you got to with the case."

I informed her of how the poison had been found in Father Michael's special supply of tea, and explained in detail the interviews with Mrs Brown, Betty and Alfie Dawkins. Over coffee and a digestif in the sitting room, my aunt gave me her thoughts.

"From what you tell me it's looking increasingly worse for Mrs Blenkinsop. She had the means at her disposal in the form of the poisonous seeds, more than enough opportunity with both her work at the church and as the vicar's house-keeper, and now it seems you've discovered the motive. Her affair with the groom should it come to light would mean the loss of everything she holds dear, her marriage, her children, not to mention her reputation. It was Father Michael who discovered them together and now he's been murdered. But even in the face of all this you're still not convinced she's guilty, are you?"

"No, I'm not. It's all circumstantial at best, and if you take Jocasta out of the picture as a suspect then I think it could quite easily be someone else who killed Father Michael."

"Well, who are your other suspects?"

"There is no one else unfortunately. But why wait so long to get rid of him if he posed such a threat? He discovered her infidelity last September, yet he wasn't killed until the following May."

"But he had been away for most of that time, had he not? Perhaps this was his reason for going, he needed time to think what he should do about his discovery. Perhaps he approached her on his return and told her his conscience wouldn't allow him to remain silent? Remember, Ella, lust is one of the seven deadly sins and each one goes against the root of Christianity. Adultery wouldn't be something Father Michael would take lightly."

"No, of course it wouldn't, but I feel as though I'm missing some crucial clue. Doesn't it seem a little too convenient that someone would break into Jocasta's greenhouse and steal the poisonous seeds? Then there is the tea. It's a Carnaby's blend, did I tell you that?"

"Yes, you did, but it's delivered countrywide, Ella. In fact

I hear they may soon start supplying some of the larger London department stores, it's very popular."

"What can you tell me about them? Would it be possible, for instance, to poison the tea prior to it being shipped out?"

"I sincerely doubt it. The company is owned by the Fortnum brothers, whom I happen to know quite well, and the entire process is a heavily guarded secret. I've had the privilege of touring the factory and believe me the security is akin to that of the palace. No it's entirely impossible for someone to have tampered with it there."

"Well, I suppose that means it was someone either with legitimate access or who broke into the vicarage... Oh, my goodness, I've just remembered something."

I stood up and began to pace while I put my thoughts in order. Occasionally glancing at Phantom who was sitting staring at the black cat in the painting Pierre DuPont had gifted me.

"Aunt Margaret, do you remember me telling you I nearly ran over Agnes outside of St Mary's?"

"I do."

"Well, that was the first time we met. I also met Jocasta for the first time then too."

"Yes, and you helped with the flower arrangements, correct?"

"That's right, but we also had several hot drinks. It was so cold in the meeting room as the boiler had broken down and we needed something to warm us up. However, the tea had run out so Jocasta pinched some from the vicarage. Agnes and I had coffee but Jocasta drank the vicar's tea. However the most important clue is that she was perfectly fine afterwards."

"So it didn't contain poison then," my aunt said, quickly grasping onto the salient point.

"Exactly. But a few days later at the meeting for the fete committee, Agnes was terribly upset as she had forgotten to purchase more tea, so once again Jocasta purloined some from the vicarage. I remember quite clearly there were only three people who drank the tea that night. Jocasta, Anne, and Mrs Fielding."

"All of whom subsequently became quite poorly. That is very interesting, Ella."

"Isn't it? So the poison must have been introduced during the time between my first visit to St Mary's and the fete meeting. And if Jocasta knew there was Ricin in the tea then surely she would never have drunk it?"

"Well, it seems unlikely, but then again it's a clever way to cast suspicion elsewhere."

"Perhaps, but even if she was prepared to take a small amount of the poison herself, she would never risk her friends. Mrs Fielding is elderly and the poison affected her much more, she was quite seriously ill for a while. All of them have been visited by Doctor Wenhope since, and they all seem to be recovering, thank goodness."

"I think you're correct, Ella. But if Jocasta didn't poison the tea then who on earth did? And more to the point, why?"

The next morning with nothing much to keep me occupied until Baxter and I went to the train station to collect Jocasta, my aunt and I took a leisurely breakfast together then a walk around the garden.

"I'll be leaving tomorrow morning, Ella. And before you say anything I genuinely have had a lovely time. The cottage is adorable and the island quite enchanting, in fact I shall be visiting more often from now on."

"You know you're welcome any time, Aunt Margaret, it's been wonderful having you here, even though I've not spent as much time with you as I would have liked. Oh, and while I remember please do thank your housekeeper for the donations, it was very generous of her."

"I will. She'll be pleased to know they were such a valuable contribution."

"Aunt Margaret," I said, stopping and taking both her hands, "I can't thank you enough for being here and supporting me during the last weeks. When the news of John came through it was such a shock, and I don't think I would have managed at all without you."

"Oh, my darling girl, you are my family and I love you dearly. Of course I would take care of you. I'm just glad I was here with you when it happened. But take it from me, you are stronger than you know and don't ever forget it. But by the same token, have a good cry if you feel like it, there's no sense bottling it all up. Now, is there any news on when the extension to the Church will be built?"

"I'm afraid it's all rather up in the air at present with the loss of Father Michael. Plus of course, Jocasta was steering the committee, and while you and I know what's about to happen no one else does. Without Jocasta the building may not go ahead at all."

"So you're quite sure an arrest is imminent even after what we realised last night?"

"I don't think there will be any alternative considering the mounting evidence against her, but I will bring Baxter up to date before we interview Jocasta this evening and see what his thoughts are. I'm rather hoping we can avoid putting her in prison while we exhaust all other avenues."

"Like a house arrest you mean?" asked my aunt.

"Yes, something like that. Of course it will all depend on what she says. If she does break down and confess well..."

"She'll only do that if she is guilty and you've quite swayed me to your way of thinking, my dear. She does have much to lose but I'm not wholly certain she would commit murder to save it. What do you know of her husband? Could he have found out about the affair and murdered Father Michael, to save his wife?"

"It will be a question to put to her of course, but according to Alfie Dawkins, they never met unless they were absolutely certain Hubert Blenkinsop was in London. I don't see how he could have found out. But even if he did and decided not to confront his wife about it, how would he know the vicar had been a witness? No, the more I think about it the more

I'm convinced that he was unaware of their liaisons."

"So we're back to square one with Jocasta being the only viable suspect," my aunt said with a sigh.

"I'm afraid we are."

At four thirty on the dot that evening, Baxter and I were sitting in the car at the station waiting for the four forty-five from Waterloo. I'd explained the poison had been added to the tea in between my first two visits to St Mary's, and who had drunk it.

"So we could easily 'ave been investigatin' four suspicious deaths rather than just one?" he said with a disbelieving shake of his head.

"Yes. Including that of our prime suspect. I've taken the liberty of speaking with Doctor Wenhope to confirm poison. He has been treating them all anyway, but he'll do some follow up visits now he has a correct diagnosis. However, he told me he thought the danger had passed so they must all have only ingested a small quantity. When he said that I realised he was right. At the fete meeting I distinctly remember Anne adding so much milk to her cup there was barely room for the tea. Mrs fielding drank just under half and then spilled the rest, and Jocasta was so busy talking she barely drunk any."

He made some notes in his little book as I stared out of the window watching a car pull up and park not far from where we were.

"I say, isn't that Jocasta's driver?" I asked.

Baxter glanced at the car and nodded.

"It is. I'll go and 'ave a word while you go to the platform to meet Mrs Blenkinsop."

A few minutes later the train pulled into the little station amid gusts of billowing steam and Jocasta stepped down lightly onto the platform, an overnight bag in her hand.

"Jocasta," I called, and standing on tiptoe waved over the heads of the alighting crowd.

"Ella, what a nice surprise. What are you doing here?"

"I've come to meet you."

"You have? Well, that's very thoughtful but how did you know I'd be here?"

"I spoke to your housekeeper yesterday and she mentioned it. Come along, the car is this way," I said and quickened my step in an attempt to avoid more questions.

We walked through the station building and out the other side towards the car, where Jocasta immediately spied my companion leaning against the door. Her countenance stiffened slightly and a wary look appeared in her eye briefly, but she carried on gamely.

"And Sergeant Baxter too. Well, what a welcome committee, I feel quite honoured."

"Mrs Blenkinsop," Baxter said in greeting, and helped her into the rear of the vehicle.

Once we were all settled I set off towards Briarlea.

"So how was London?" I asked.

"Busy, noisy and quite dirty. It's easy to forget all that discord exists when living here, it catches me by surprise every time I go."

"Was it a special occasion?"

"The birthday of a friend of my husband's. Dinner, theatre and dancing, the usual sort of thing when you go to the city."

"It sounds wonderful," I said.

"Yes, it does, doesn't it?" she replied in a way that made me think she hadn't enjoyed it at all. "So why are you really here? I assume you have news of Father Michael's death?" she continued.

"That's right, Mrs Blenkinsop. There's some new information come to light and we wanted to keep you updated," answered Baxter smoothly, while my stomach churned.

"I see. Well we can speak in the drawing room, we won't be disturbed there."

"Can I get you a drink of something?" Jocasta asked as we settled into the drawing room.

She approached the drinks cabinet and after some musing decided on a stiff gin and tonic. Baxter and I both declined the offer of alcohol.

"But I wouldn't say no to a coffee if there is one?" Baxter said.

Jocasta rang the bell and a moment later a butler appeared.

"You rang, madam?"

"Yes, could you ask Tilly to bring coffee please."

"Certainly, madam," replied the butler and with a stiff bow disappeared.

Leaning against the sill of the large window, glass in hand, Jocasta turned to face us.

"So what is this new information you mentioned in the car?"

Baxter cleared his throat, then said, "We spoke with Alfie Dawkins yesterday, Mrs Blenkinsop. We know about yer affair."

I watched Jocasta like a hawk as this news was imparted but she remained quite still, staring into midair but seemingly seeing nothing, her face inscrutable. Eventually she took a sip of her drink and turned to look out of the window.

"It was only a matter of time before you found out, I suppose."

"Do you understand the implications of this, Mrs Blenkinsop?" Baxter asked.

"I'm not a fool, Sergeant Baxter," she said softly. "Of course I understand. It's a motive."

At that inopportune moment there was a knock at the door, and the maid entered with the coffee.

"Just put it on the table, Tilly," instructed Jocasta.

Tilly did as she was told, then quietly retreated.

Still intent on the view of the terrace and gardens beyond the window, Jocasta began to speak in quiet tones as though to herself.

"Have you ever felt as though you were a stranger in your own life? Going about things day to day but never really feeling as though you belong? Practically invisible but for a series of titles and associated duties; wife, mother, Mrs Blenkinsop, but never Jocasta, never me. No one ever saw me until Alfie. You've met him of course so you understand what a remarkable young man he is. An old soul in a young body is how I referred to him. He understood me better than anyone else ever has and immediately saw how lonely I was."

She sighed heavily and took another sip of her drink. I saw Baxter put down his notebook and take a breath and quickly stayed his arm before he spoke. He looked at me quizzically and I gave a slight shake of my head. I realised this was the first time Jocasta had ever spoken so openly and I didn't want any interruptions. She would get to the point eventually but it was important she got to it in her own way, regardless of how roundabout it was. Baxter seemed to realise what I meant and settled back with his coffee as Jocasta continued.

"I married too young, you see, to a man who was a friend of my father's and twice my age. And while it was quite wonderful in the beginning it didn't take me long to realise what a horrible mistake I had made. But of course by then it was too late, we already had one child and the second was about to be born. With two sons, Hubert had done his duty and his life was once more his own. It was the oddest feeling but I felt like a widow even though he was still alive. For the sake of the boys we've kept up appearances but the marriage has been over for a long time now."

She shook her head and realising her glass was empty went to refill it.

"But of course you want to know about Father Michael. I wasn't one hundred percent sure he had seen us that day, you know. I saw him cycling away but that wasn't to say he'd stopped by the stables. I became certain, however, the following Sunday when the subject of his sermon was sins of the flesh, he looked at me directly several times and I knew without a doubt he'd been there. So I waited until the service was over and everyone had left, then I went to speak with him in private."

"You did?" I asked, momentarily forgetting my decision to keep quiet at this revelation.

"I can see you're surprised at the news, but it wasn't as though it would make any difference. My marriage was already over, Alfie had gone and our affair ended, it was the right time to clear the air. My only concern was for my children and I knew Father Michael would never speak of our conversation."

"But 'ow could you be so sure?" asked Baxter.

"Because it happened within the sanctity of a confessional, Sergeant, and he would have been prohibited from repeating it."

"So you see I had absolutely no reason to kill Father Michael as my secrets were safe," Jocasta continued. "I will also tell you plainly now that I did not do so, you will need to look elsewhere to find your murderer. However, there is something else I can tell you that may be of help."

"And what is that, Mrs Blenkinsop?" asked Baxter retrieving his notebook.

"The father and I talked briefly after we had left the confessional, and he appeared to me to be quite overwhelmed with worry about another matter entirely. Eventually after some gentle encouragement he intimated he had recently lost a friend, a man he had held in great esteem. I could see he blamed himself but I didn't understand exactly why until he said, 'The devil comes in many guises, if only I'd recognised sooner he'd taken her to his side he might still be alive.' And that was it. After that he made me promise not to give in to further temptation and seek forgiveness from God. Which I did."

We sat in silence for a moment while Baxter and I digested this information.

"What do you believe he meant by that, Mrs Blenkinsop?"

"Well, I'm no detective but, and I've thought about it quite a lot since, I think he had information about a crime against a man he considered a friend, by a woman he knew. Possibly a spouse and probably a murder. Father Michael hadn't been here long, remember, so I'm quite sure it must have happened in his previous parish, although where that was I haven't the foggiest. But I think this must have been the reason he left and why his previous posting was deliberately kept quiet."

Baxter and I excused ourselves while we went out through the French windows onto the terrace. We needed to discuss this new information further and in private.

"Do you think she's telling the truth? We only 'ave her word the conversation with the vicar took place," Baxter said as we sauntered to the end of the terrace where we could still see Jocasta seated in the drawing room, but wouldn't be over-heard.

"Well, I'm considered a bit of an expert at spotting the art of a lie. Oh! That's perfect," I said scrabbling in my bag for my notebook.

"What is?"

"It's the perfect title for the compendium, The Art of the Lie, especially with your wonderful illustrations. I knew it would come to me eventually."

"I see. But do you think we could get back to the case?" Baxter asked, smirking.

"Of course. Well, I have to say I do think she's telling the truth, there were no indications of subterfuge in her man-nerisms, and what's more I don't think she murdered Father Michael. However, as she is our only suspect I'll understand if you want to arrest her, although I'd prefer it if you didn't. I'm not sure her reputation would ever recover if she's hauled in for killing a priest even if she is subsequently found inno-cent. It hardly seems fair to do that to her."

Baxter looked at me in amusement.

"And what would you suggest instead?"

"Well I was talking to Aunt Margaret about it last night..."

"You were, were you?"

"Yes, she's an extremely good listener and very clever at this sort of thing. I wondered if some sort of house arrest would be an option? Perhaps we could arrange for a plain clothes detective to stay here for a while under the guise of a family friend to save face, while we follow this new lead?"

Baxter laughed.

"Well, you've certainly thought this through, I'll give you that, and it might be possible, but I'll have to speak to my superiors, it's a bit above my pay grade. 'Owever, there's a bit of a problem as far as I can see."

"Oh?"

"Just where exactly is this new lead?"

I sat on the terrace wall thoroughly deflated. Without the Archbishop of York, who was not due back for a while, we had no idea where the vicar's previous parish had been. With such little factual information to go on it would be impossible to know where to start.

"I suppose the only thing we can do is to petition the church for the information. They've obviously kept things quiet to protect Father Michael, but now he's dead I don't suppose they'll mind sharing what they know. But I have no idea how to go about it, have you?" I asked Baxter.

"None whatsoever, and my Super is dealin' with that side anyway. But I'll speak to 'im when I call about the plain clothes man we need 'ere. Come on, we'd better tell Mrs Blenkinsop what we're planning."

Jocasta greeted the news of her house arrest and the presence of a plain clothes detective living in her house with incredible grace.

"I wouldn't have gone anywhere of course, there's nowhere for me to go, and I must be here for the boys, they need their mother. But I do understand until the real killer is found this is the best option, and I appreciate you taking my feelings and reputation into consideration."

"Will yer husband be agreeable?" asked Baxter.

Jocasta sighed and rose once more to stand at the window.

"I very much doubt he'll find out, Sergeant. You see I asked him for a divorce while we were in London and he said yes. I'm quite sure there is a mistress or two in the city who will jump at the chance to take my place."

I expressed my sorrow at her news but she waved my comment away.

"Don't worry, Ella, it's something we should have done a long time ago. At least now I'll have the chance to be happy in the future. Now is there anything else?"

"There is just one thing, then p'raps I could use yer telephone?" said Baxter.

"Of course there's one in the hall."

"Much obliged. Now, can you tell me who knew you kept poisonous seeds on the premises?"

"Goodness, probably the whole village, if not the entire island. I speak at the Linhay Horticultural Society quite often, you see, and always take samples of seeds and plants with me. It's held at the village hall and is always full to capacity."

Baxter sighed and I saw he scribbled, 'between four and eight thousand depending on time of year,' in his book. The population practically doubled when the tourist season was upon us and I realised it would be impossible to follow this line of inquiry.

"Thank you, Mrs Blenkinsop. I'll use the telephone now."

I took the opportunity to use the powder room while Baxter was making calls and returned mere moments before he did.

"Right, that's all sorted. There'll be a plain clothes man arriving at Linhay train station at ten tomorrow mornin'. He is to be yer third cousin twice removed on yer mother's side. Name o' Charles. I trust yer driver can pick 'im up?"

"I'll see to the arrangements after you've left, and thank you both again," Jocasta said as she showed us out.

"So they're gettin' a divorce. A sad business. I only 'ope it works out the way she wants it to. While the grass might be green on the other side of the fence she may well find it's no greener than what she has now, only a different shade," Baxter said as we got in the car.

"Or she could discover a verdant oasis where she is no longer invisible and taken for granted," I said.

"Well, there's always that I suppose, and I agree she 'as been treated a bit shabbily by 'er husband if what she says is true. Well we've done all we can 'ere fer now, if you could take me to the station I'm headed back to London. Apparently there's a mountain of paperwork to complete fer the acquisition of a plain clothes baby sitter."

I smiled at Baxter's faux grumpiness, then putting the car into gear started the journey to the railway station. As I drove, my thoughts turned to how little real progress we were making on the case. If the church were unable or unwilling to give us the information we needed then we would soon find ourselves with no way of moving forward, and that worried me greatly. However the elusive memory, a vital clue I had been chasing for days, was about to make itself known, and it came from a source I had been unwittingly ignoring; my dear cat Phantom.

Chapter TEN

EARLY THE NEXT MORNING I took Aunt Margaret to the station where she had a ticket booked on the first train out.

"Thank you, darling, it's been wonderful. I should be back home in time for afternoon tea, I'll telephone you to let you know. Best of luck with the investigation, it will all work itself out soon you'll see. And do keep me posted on developments if you can."

"I do hope you're right, Aunt Margaret, we seem to have reached a brick wall at present."

"Well, you know where I am if you want to talk things through."

A shrill whistle and clouds of steam signalled the train's imminent departure, and I stood back as the wheels began to turn and the train chugged slowly out of the station. Aunt Margaret slid down the window and waved briefly before disappearing into her carriage.

My next few hours at home were filled with tasks I needed to catch up on, 'The Art of the Lie,' was coming along nicely and Mrs Shaw wholeheartedly agreed with the new title. I caught up on some correspondence then took a walk in the gardens.

It was a beautiful summer day with a clear blue sky and not a cloud in sight. I hadn't seen Tom for days but he'd managed to clear an impressive amount of dead shrubbery along the wall of the enclosed garden, and eventually a large wooden gate had been revealed. It was terribly exciting but I was under strict instructions not to interfere, and I was quite happy to leave him to it. The key to the gate had been unearthed in one of the out-buildings, and I could hear Tom's cheerful whistle now, alongside the excited yips of Digger his little dog, emanating from beyond the wall as they worked.

I spent a very pleasant half hour sitting on the bench at the end of the garden, watching a pair of swans glide majestically up and down the river, and several ducks waddling in the reed bed on the opposite bank. I could hear a woodpecker hard at work on one of the trees in the woodland across the water, and to my immense joy a sleek otter popped his head out of a cleverly concealed holt for a moment, then vanished as quickly as he'd appeared. It was quite the most perfect and magical time with thoughts of murder pushed to the far recesses of my mind, and I felt quite rejuvenated by the time I returned to the cottage.

It was early afternoon, I'd taken my coffee into the sitting room and once again I found Phantom staring at the painting from Pierre.

"Dear, Phantom, I realise that you cats were worshiped as Gods by the early Egyptians, but this really is taking your narcissistic tendencies a little too far, don't you think?" I said to him as I moved closer to study the painting in more detail. "Although I do agree it is a very good likeness... Oh!"

I barely noticed the coffee cup slip from my hands and crash to the hearth breaking into smithereens, as the elusive clue finally rushed forward to the forefront of my mind.

"Oh, Phantom, you've been trying to tell me for days, haven't you?"

Phantom finally looked at me then jumping down from his perch disappeared through the wall into the garden. His job was done.

"Miss Bridges, are you all right, I heard a crash?" Mrs Shaw said as she rushed into the room.

"I'm fine, Mrs Shaw, I just dropped the coffee cup. Sorry, I need to call my aunt urgently."

"Actually that's what I was coming to tell you when I heard the crash. She's on the telephone now."

"She is? Goodness, she seems to be able to read my mind from a distance too," I murmured, dashing into the hall and picking up the receiver.

"Aunt Margaret, I need..."

"Ella, listen to me, you need to come at once. I've just spoken to my housekeeper."

"That's just what I was going to say."

"It was?"

"Yes, and I'll be bringing Sergeant Baxter."

"I was going to suggest that myself."

"I also need you to do something for me."

I explained to my aunt what I wanted and she agreed immediately.

"What time will you be here?" she asked.

"I'll telephone Baxter now and ask him to meet me off the train at Waterloo, but it will be quite late. I doubt we'll get to Broughton station much before eleven tonight."

"My driver will be waiting for you both. I'll see you soon, Ella."

I telephoned Baxter as soon as I had disconnected from Aunt Margaret, and once I had briefly explained how the pieces were finally fitting together he agreed to the journey at once.

"That's an excellent bit o' detective work, Miss Bridges, well done. But time is of the essence if what yer tellin' me is right, and a man's life is at stake. I'll get a plain clothes man to get over there and watch the 'ouse urgently. See you soon."

True to her word, Aunt Margaret's driver was waiting at Broughton train station when we arrived, and by eleven fifteen we were all comfortably seated in the parlour.

"Is Pierre here?" I asked.

"No, dear, you know what he's like with, er, crowds. But he sent what you asked for."

I shared a smile with my aunt, understanding immediately Pierre's reluctance to meet yet another member of Scotland Yard.

"Who's Pierre?" asked Baxter.

"Pierre DuPont." I said

"The artist? Well I never. 'Ow is he involved in this mess?"

"You've heard of him?" I said somewhat surprised.

"Indeed I 'ave. I've long bin an admirer of 'is work, Miss Bridges. Once upon a time I fancied I'd be lucky enough to own one of 'is paintings, sadly the more popular they are the further out o' my reach. But 'ow on earth is he involved with this case?"

Aunt Margaret interrupted at this point.

"Before you get to that would you mind listening to what my housekeeper has to say? The poor dear has been waiting up for you."

Mrs Shipley came into the parlour, full of her usual cheeriness and bright smile, despite the lateness of the hour.

"Miss Isobella, how lovely to see you again so soon."

"Hello, Mrs Shipley. This is Sergeant Baxter."

She greeted Baxter then at my aunt's urging began her tale.

"When your aunt returned home this afternoon she passed on your thanks regarding the donations for your May Day fete. You are very welcome, by the way. Now I believe she told you we wouldn't be needing them this year but not why?"

"I wasn't aware of it until you told me today," said my aunt.

"No, I realise that, I apologise," said the housekeeper.

"No need to apologise, Shipley, I was just explaining for Ella and Sergeant Baxter."

"Do go on, Mrs Shipley." I said.

"Well, the reason we no longer needed them was because we weren't having a fair this year, because our vicar had left unexpectedly. It was at the end of July last year and he just up and disappeared, none of us had any inkling. He didn't even say goodbye. We all thought it terribly odd at the time. Of course there have been a number of rumours since, some complete nonsense of course, but the general consensus is that he found out something about one of the parishioners which caused him to go. But one of his friends died around the same time so it could just as easily have been that."

"Mrs Shipley, what was the name of this priest?" I asked.

"Oh, of course, I apologise. It was Father Michael."

Mrs Shipley could tell us nothing more and so retired. She didn't know who the deceased friend had been but the description she gave us of her Father Michael fitted ours perfectly, and none of us were in any doubt it was the same man.

"Well, we're certainly gettin' somewhere now," Baxter said with relief in his voice, then added... "All we need now is to find the woman Father Michael mentioned to Mrs Blenkinsop, and we should be able to wrap this case up."

"I believe I can help with that. Aunt Margaret, do you have the painting and drawings Pierre sent over?"

My aunt nodded and collected a parcel from the sideboard.

Bringing it over, she unwrapped it carefully and laid the contents on the table in front of us.

"Good god!" Baxter exclaimed, in a very unbaxterlike way.

"Awful, isn't it?" I said.

"Well, it's a remarkable bit o' work, very well done, but it is quite 'orrible. What on earth pointed you in the direction o' this?"

"My cat."

"I didn't realise you had a cat."

"Well, he's not really mine, he appears and disappears when he feels like it."

Baxter nodded knowingly. "The wife and me 'ave a stray as well, turns up when he feels like it, fer food mostly. But back to this paintin', can you explain how it all fits together? How yer've come to the conclusion you 'ave?"

"Well, it all started when I came to visit Aunt Margaret the other week and we visited Pierre DuPont's gallery."

"He 'as a gallery here?" asked Baxter with extreme interest.

"He does, and no doubt you'll be able to visit tomorrow. Anyway it just so happened this painting was in the window. It wasn't supposed to be, Pierre was quite cross when he realised and removed it at once. But of course I'd seen it by then and once seen never forgotten, however it got pushed to the back of my mind until I received your note with the drawings for the compendium."

"Right. And 'ow did that 'elp exactly?"

"Your note mentioned you'd gone out and drawn real people.

I've never really thought how artists paint their subjects before, but of course it must be like that. Regardless, it suddenly dawned on me you'd need to have a real person to sketch to start with."

"And you think Mr DuPont based this paintin' on a real person?"

"Oh, I'm sure of it, I recognise her, you see. But I asked him to also send preliminary sketches if he had any just to make sure. I presume those are in this portfolio."

I untied the ribbon holding the portfolio together and opened it with extreme care, the sketches as well as the painting itself were worth a lot of money. Inside were several loose sheets of paper each with numerous pencil studies of the same woman.

"Yes, this is definitely her. I thought originally I must have seen her at St Mary's but it was one of those elusive memories that I couldn't quite grasp. I realise now the painting was what I was remembering."

"But this is your suspect?" asked my aunt.

"Yes, it is. You see I've met her since on Linhay."

"So you know who she is?"

"I know who she is now, but not who she was when she lived here and that's the proof we need. Did you ask Pierre those questions I gave you on the phone when we spoke earlier, Aunt Margaret?"

"I did and I wrote down his answers."

She reached over to retrieve a writing pad and tearing off the top sheet handed it to me. Baxter and I read in silence for a moment.

"I'll visit this place Nell Bank tomorrow," Baxter said pointing at one of the answers.

"My driver can drop Ella and myself in town then be at your disposal for the rest of the day, Sergeant. You'll have the furthest of all of us to travel," Aunt Margaret offered. "Now I think we'd better turn in, it's very late and we have an exceedingly busy day ahead of us tomorrow."

She was right, for if everything went according to plan, tomorrow we would catch a murderer.

The next morning was a flurry of activity as Aunt Margaret, Baxter and myself made our plans. Baxter was to go to an address at Nell Bank to see if he could obtain both a name and more information, then onto the local police station to discuss a suspicious death. After that he would visit a company of solicitors in Sheffield, the address of which I had given him previously.

Aunt Margaret was to visit the local paper, to read any applicable news reports in archived publications around the time of Father Michael's disappearance. And I was to return Pierre's artwork and to see if he could give us anything more about the muse he used for his painting, 'From Mistress to Wife.'

We would all meet up later at the art gallery.

I waved goodbye as the car containing my Aunt and Baxter drove away, then with the little bell signalling my arrival entered the premises.

I was greeted by a tall heavyset girl in a black dress with white apron, and a mass of blond hair piled on top of her head in a complicated arrangement of thick plaits. Which gave the impression she wore an upturned wicker basket on her head. Blue eyes the size of dinner plates turned to greet me and a smile broke out through rose-coloured lips which lit up her whole face and made her eyes shine in a remarkably mischievous way.

"Good morning, welcome to the DuPont Gallery. May I be of assistance?"

"I'm here to see Monsieur DuPont. My name is Ella Bridges."

Before the girl could reply the man himself appeared from beyond the curtain. He was wearing a floor length apron which was so covered in splotches of paint it was difficult to know what its original colour had been. Upon his head was a French beret in midnight blue velvet, and he had a paintbrush stuck behind one ear.

"Meez Bridges, how deeelightful to see you again," he said as he bowed to kiss my hand.

"Bonjour, Pierre."

"Hilda, bring tea immediately. We will take it in the studio. Chop chop," he said, clapping his hands.

Hilda rolled her eyes and with a smile at me said to the little man, "Be polite or I shall hide your ladders."

I stifled a surprised laugh as she disappeared toward the kitchen. Pierre took my elbow and gently steered me toward the back room, shaking his head in mock exasperation.

"Mon Dieu! But it is difficult to get good staff nowadays."

Safely seated in the studio, which to my eye was every bit as confusing and disorganised as the shop, and with tea on a low table in front of us, I explained the reason for my visit.

"Firstly, I would like to thank you for the loan of your painting and sketches."

"Think nothing of it. Were they of help?"

"Very much so. Indeed your paintings have provided a vital thread throughout this latest case."

"And just what is this case you speak of?"

"Murder, Pierre. I am investigating a murder."

"Sacre bleu! But this is most horrible to hear, Maggie mentioned nothing of this on the telephone. And you wish for my help in some way? But what can I do? I know nothing of this murder?"

"Can you tell me more about the woman you used for this painting?" I asked, indicating the two-faced woman which I had unwrapped and placed on a convenient easel just moments earlier.

"It is she who is dead? Ah, no... I see now, it is she who is the culprit, no?"

I nodded.

"It does not surprise me so much actually. You can see how I painted her, so different from my usual work, yes? This is how she appeared to me, beautiful to look at but with a core of evil and rotten to her soul."

"Can you tell me from the beginning how you came to meet her?"

"Of course, but I did not really meet her until a long time after the portrait was finished, when she visited the shop unexpectedly. But I will begin at the beginning and tell you what little I can."

Pierre's tale began on a warm day in Spring of the previous year. With an urge for fresh air he'd taken his sketch book and pencils to a little park opposite St. Paul's church in Broughton, and had settled himself to an afternoon of sketching. He had been there perhaps two hours, and filled several pages with drawings when this woman had appeared and sat on a nearby bench. At first he'd simply watched her, she seemingly oblivious to his attentions, then he felt a compulsion so strong to immortalise her he became almost afraid. But he was powerless to the stop the impulse and page after page he filled with her image, pencil flying over the paper as though with a life of its own. Eventually, much later and completely exhausted he had laid down his pencil and closed his eyes.

"When I opened them she was standing but a short distance away, observing me," he said with a shudder.

"What did she say?" I asked.

"Nothing at all, but her face for an instant... malfaisant! You understand? It was pure evil. Then the mask came down again and she simply turned and walked away."

"Had she seen your drawings?"

"I'm sure of it."

"What happened then?"

"I gathered up my work and proceeded in the same direction."

"You followed her? Why?"

"Alas I do not know. It was as though my actions were not my own, like being a puppet whose strings were being manipulated from elsewhere. I have never felt anything like it before or since, and I never wish to again. It sounds fanciful, does it not? But it is as exactly as I have explained."

Pierre had continued to follow the woman unobserved to an affluent part of the town, where she had disappeared through the gate of a large house.

"Nell Bank," I said.

"Oui, just like I told Maggie."

"So when did she come to the shop?"

"Not until June. It was a horrible shock to hear the little bell then find her standing there. She demanded to see the painting I had done of her. I had finished it of course but I told her it did not exist. That I had returned with the sketches but they had amounted to nothing."

"And did she believe you?"

Pierre gave a shrug.

"I did not know and I did not care. I offered to give her something else instead and when she informed me of the illness of her husband, I found something suitable and she left. I have never seen her again."

"This is why you were upset the day I came to find Hilda had displayed the painting in the window?"

"But of course. I had lied and said it did not exist. What would have happened if she had seen it?"

"You have no more need to worry, Pierre. She no longer lives in Broughton, she has moved to Linhay."

"Such a relief I cannot tell you!"

"I'm glad you are relieved and thank you for telling me it all. I realise it must have been quite an ordeal. Now I need to tell you my aunt will be here shortly along with my colleague."

"Another policeman?"

"Yes. I thought I should tell you in case... well, never mind. But he is a great fan of your work and has been looking forward to visiting the gallery and meeting you."

"Then we shall make him feel quite at home, mon amie."

The bell above the shop door tinkled the arrival of newcomers, and a moment later Hilda popped her head through the curtain.

"Visitors to see you, Oh Mighty One," she said with a cheeky glint in her eye.

"Less of your impudence, wench, or you will find yourself on the streets," Pierre replied.

"Yes, My Lord," said the girl with a giggle, and disappeared back into the shop.

Chapter ELEVEN

"AH, MAGGIE, YOU LOOK AS LOVELY AS EVER," Pierre said with a bow and a kiss of her hand. "And this must be the colleague of Miss Bridges, no?"

"Sergeant Baxter, Mr DuPont. It is a real pleasure to meet you at last."

"Likewise, my dear Sergeant. Now, say nothing more!"

Aunt Margaret and I stood to one side while Pierre dragged his stepladders in front of Baxter, and peered deeply into his eyes. Baxter shot a worried glance at me and his eyebrows rose high enough to disappear beneath his hairline, as a blush crept across his cheeks. I couldn't help but grin.

"Mmmm. Most interesting," the dwarf said.

Grasping Baxter's hands he turned them this way and that, examining them first close up, then at a distance.

"Yes, it is as I thought. Remain still please."

Jumping off the ladder he wandered around the perplexed

sergeant, studying him from every angle until he declared himself done.

"A man after my own heart. I have the most perfect piece for you, my dear Sergeant."

I had assumed it would take some time, as it had with me, for Pierre to find a gift for Baxter. But I was wrong. With a flourish he pulled a small frame from the rear of the chaise-longue just seconds later.

"Eh voila!" he said and thrust the painting into Baxter's hands.

"Well, I never. How did you know?" he said, staring at Pierre in astonishment.

"What is it? Do let me see," I said, moving to Baxter's side.

The painting was exquisite. A small tow-headed boy sitting on the stoop of a step, his tongue caught between his teeth and a look of fierce concentration on his face as he bent over a little drawing pad, sketching in perfect detail a Robin Redbreast perched atop a milk bottle.

"It's simply perfect, isn't it?" I said.

He looked at me with a questioning raise of an eyebrow.

"I never said a word, Baxter. Truly."

"Then how?" he said, once again addressing Pierre.

The little man gave a depreciating shrug.

"It is easy to identify a fellow artiste. Would you not agree? Now I'll have Hilda wrap it for you."

As we were leaving Baxter turned to the dwarf and shook his hand.

"It's been a real pleasure to meet you, Mr DuPont. I'm more grateful than words can say. If there is ever anything I can do fer yer in return..."

"As a matter of fact, there is something, Sergeant."

"Yes?"

"Catch this despicable murderess, for she is evil through and through."

"I 'ave every intention of doing so, sir. You can count on it."

"I presume my aunt told you to accept a gift from Pierre if he offered?" I asked Baxter as we settled in the car.

"Yes indeed, said he'd feel mortally wounded if I refused, 'though she warned me it might not 'appen. He's very particular 'bout who he gifts his paintings to, I feel very honoured."

My Aunt nodded.

"Perfectly true, it's very rare for him to bestow his work on strangers and you have both been honoured. He must think highly of you."

"How does he do it, Aunt Margaret? Find the most perfect painting for the person?"

"Honestly I have no idea, darling. He says it's a gift and I don't question it. Now I thought we'd visit the tea rooms on the way home and discuss our findings. There are some private booths at the rear which will be perfect for our needs. I find myself in dire need of sustenance."

Ensconced in a booth at the rear of The Lilly Tearooms, the table groaning with more food than the three of us could possibly eat, we shared what we had learned.

I began by relaying the story Pierre had told me, how he'd eventually followed our suspect to a large house at Nell Bank and culminating in her visit to his shop some months later.

"Goodness, poor Pierre. I had no idea," my aunt said.

"How did you get on at the newspaper?" I asked.

"Quite well, as a matter of fact. I only found the one article pertaining to a gentleman's suspicious death at the correct time, a man by the name of Redmond. Here, I was able to clip it."

She laid the newspaper clipping on the table and Baxter and I quickly read it.

"Not much to go on 'ere, but it mentions he lived at Nell Bank, so it must be the same man," said Baxter.

"Well, I also managed to find the reporter and he was much more forthcoming."

"That's excellent work, tracking down the reporter," said Baxter.

"Well, I'd like to take credit, Sergeant, but sadly I cannot. It's a small town newspaper and there are actually only two reporters. Both of whom happened to be in the office when I arrived, so it was quite simple to find the right one."

"Was 'is name Briggs, by any chance?"

"Why yes, it was. How did you know?"

"And did you explain yer were workin' with a Scotland Yard detective who was at that very moment on 'is way to Nell Bank?"

"Of course, I could hardly waltz in there asking questions without some form of legitimacy."

"And after you imparted this information did he then excuse himself to make a brief telephone call?"

"Sergeant Baxter, you really are quite the tease. Who did he telephone?"

"The daughter from Mr Redmond's first marriage. She was waitin' outside the 'ouse when I arrived."

"So all my snooping was superfluous?"

"On the contrary, it was invaluable. 'Ow else could we 'ave flushed out the daughter? But I apologise for interruptin', please carry on."

My aunt, quite amused at Baxter, continued.

"I have made some notes of the pertinent facts..."

She informed us Mr Redmond was a man who had always been in excellent health. He had a love of the outdoors and was involved in various gentlemanly sports such as shooting and fishing. He was a regular member of St Paul's church, a keen gardener and had won many a rosette for his produce at various village shows. All this, until a fall had necessitated a hospital stay for a broken leg, after which he had never quite fully recovered. But according to the reporter Briggs, he had fallen in love with his young nurse and married her not long after his release.

"After that he became almost a recluse apparently. I also managed to obtain this, it's the original from the newspaper so I will need to return it, but this is Mr Redmond."

Aunt Margaret handed us a photograph, as soon as I saw it

the connections became clear and I knew we had the murderer in our sights. It was of an elderly man in tweeds with a cane, standing in front of a floral display and holding up a first prize rosette. My aunt also had another interesting morsel to share.

"Mr Redmond had a hothouse and grew many interesting specimens. Some of which were poisonous."

At this point I began to panic that we may be too late.

"Baxter, we need to move on this now before there is another death. We can't get back to Linhay in time, so you must make some telephone calls."

"Miss Bridges, no need to fret it's already in 'hand. By the time I had spoken to the solicitor I knew we 'ad our murderer, so made haste to Broughton police station where I made the calls and put things into action. I daresay there's already bin an arrest. I also made sure Doctor Wenhope was present and informed it were likely a case of prolonged poisoning he'd need to treat. I expect there'll be a message left at your Aunt's 'ouse when we return."

"Oh, thank goodness."

"'Ow did you know about the Will, by the way?" Baxter asked.

"I saw a letter when I visited. I didn't know it was about a Will at the time of course, but as things went on I remembered it because it was from Sheffield."

"Well, we've done all we can. I only 'ope we were in time to save 'im," said Baxter.

I fervently prayed we were too.

There was indeed a message at Aunt Margaret's when the three of us returned. The arrest had gone according to plan and the poisoned victim had been rushed to hospital. It was touch and go as to whether he would make it, but he was under the best care possible and it was now in the lap of the Gods.

The packets of seeds stolen from Mrs Blenkinsop's greenhouse had been found on the premises, along with a copy of a new Last Will and Testament giving everything over to the murderer. And fingerprints taken had matched those on the box of tea at the vicarage.

By the time I returned home the news of the arrest had spread through the village like wildfire, and everywhere I went shocked locals and visitors alike were huddled in small clusters discussing the news in hushed tones.

Jocasta had telephoned to inform me her resident detective had left, and to thank me again for my tact. And Agnes, in an unusual show of fortitude, had called and asked if she could come for lunch. I had naturally said yes and she appeared on time and with a freshly baked peach tart.

"Mrs Whittingstall!" exclaimed Agnes as she sat across from me at the outdoor table.

It was another beautiful day and I had decided the informal setting of the garden and dining al fresco was a perfect idea.

"I simply can't believe it. It's such a shock. But tell me, Ella, how on earth did you put it all together?"

"Well, it all started when I happened to see a ghastly painting on a visit to Aunt Margaret a few weeks ago. It's very difficult to describe to one who hasn't seen it but suffice to say it lingered in my memory."

"And this was your first clue?"

"It was, although I didn't realise it at the time, nor for quite a while actually, but that's by the by. Do you remember when you and I first met, Agnes, we were leaving St Mary's and a woman rushed down the path and bumped into me?"

"Yes it was Mrs Whittingstall, so I found out later."

"Well, I happened to look back at the church that day; it seemed to me as though she were running away from something. What I saw was Father Michael and he looked in a state of shock. Of course I realise now they must have recognised one another."

"From when he was at the Broughton Parish, you mean?"

"Quite right. You said yourself you'd never seen Mrs Whittingstall at St. Mary's prior to that incident and Father Michael had been away for a long time, returning just moments before in fact. I doubt either of them realised the other was now living on Linhay. It must have been a dreadful shock for both of them to come to face to face that day, and I'm afraid the vicar was in terrible danger from that moment on."

"But how did you know it was Mrs Whittingstall who had murdered Father Michael?"

"Well, it was a case of lots of little things which eventually made me see the bigger picture. Much of it when you and I went to visit her actually."

"I shudder when I think of that visit, it was quite horrid.

But how did it help? We never even set foot in the door so you can't have seen much."

"I saw what I needed to, Agnes."

I explained the things I had noted. The photograph of the gentleman in tweeds with his pheasants which had turned out to be Mr Redmond, and the cane in the umbrella stand which also belonged to him, I said I had filed away for future reference, not being able to attach much significance to them there and then. Of course this was a small tarradiddle on my part, however I wasn't about to add visitations from his ghost into the conversation. But I did share my observation of the Pierre DuPont painting on the back wall, and the return address of the solicitors I had seen on the letter the postman was delivering.

"I remember you mentioning the painting, but thought you were trying to make polite conversation under remarkably strained circumstances," Agnes said.

I smiled.

"Perhaps I was at the time, but it was another little clue to add to the others. Of course the real break came when my aunt telephoned about her housekeeper and insisted Sergeant Baxter and I went up there post-haste."

I relayed to Agnes all that had gone on in Broughton and the subsequent proof we had found which led to the arrest of Elizabeth Whittingstall. Previously known as Elspeth Redmond.

"Oh dear, it's all rather dreadful, isn't it, Ella? I can't imagine what Mr Redmond's daughter must have felt not only having lost her father but her entire inheritance, including her family home to this evil woman. But how do you prove murder so long after the fact?"

I looked down wondering how to explain gently to Agnes what Baxter had told me earlier. But I need not have worried about her sensibilities as she grasped the truth almost immediately.

"He's going to be exhumed? How utterly ghastly. But I suppose it must be done for the family's sake. I wonder what actually happened between Mrs Whittingstall and Father Michael, do you know?"

I shook my head.

"I don't think we will ever know for certain, Agnes, but here is what I think happened. Mr Redmond was a good friend of Father Michael's, someone he held in great esteem and presumably spent a lot of time with. But all that changed when his new wife came on the scene and succeeded in isolating him from his family and friends. Of course we think now she was slowly poisoning him and preventing anyone from realising the truth of what was happening. Sadly she was very successful in that regard. However I believe Father Michael was suspicious and not realising how truly dangerous this woman was, eventually made a dreadful error in judgment when his friend died. He met with her and accused her face to face of murder."

'Oh dear, I'm sorry. I thought I had come to terms with it but hearing this..." said Agnes, fishing for her handkerchief as tears coursed down her cheeks.

"Don't worry, Agnes, it's delayed shock, it happens like

that, catching you unawares at the least expected moment," I said gently, taking her hand.

She nodded and blew her nose.

"Please carry on."

"Are you sure?"

"Yes, I need to know."

"All right. Well there isn't much more to tell but Sergeant Baxter is still up in Broughton and has found out something else. Shortly after the funeral of Mr Redmond, according to witnesses, his widow visited the church and went to confession. It is our belief she must have confessed to Father Michael that she had murdered her husband and..."

"He couldn't tell anyone," finished Agnes, a look of anguish on her face.

"No, he couldn't. It was a cruel and evil thing to do but she is an evil woman. I'm quite sure she deliberately told him in order to gloat and prove she had got away with it. And I'm sure this is what had been troubling him for so long and the reason he took his sabbatical."

"Why did she do it, Ella? Murder her first husband and try to murder her second?"

"For the inheritance. It was greed pure and simple."

Agnes sat back and sipped her tea in contemplative silence for a while before asking a final question.

"She won't get away with it, will she, Ella? She's going to be sent to prison for the rest of her life, isn't she?"

"She might not go to prison, Agnes. Baxter has heard

rumours of an insanity plea. If she is found to be mad then she will be incarcerated in an asylum. But you have no need to worry, I can assure you she will never be a free woman again."

Agnes nodded then, accepting of my word. I was under no such illusion, however. I felt sure a plea of insanity would be thrown out as the crimes had been premeditated, very carefully and cleverly worked out. No, Baxter and I both agreed that the reprehensible Mrs Whittingstall would be hanged from the neck until dead.

The next day I decided to ride over to St Mary's. Propping my bicycle against the wall just inside the lych-gate I walked leisurely up the path toward the entrance. I had come to light a candle for John.

He'd been buried properly this time, in the grave where I thought he had rested for the last two years. I had not been allowed to attend, done as it was under cover of darkness and in secret, however I had been assured full protocols had been observed. I frowned at the ludicrous, impersonal language which had been used, but understood it to mean a vicar had been present along with a few members of MI5 who were his friends, and a proper burial had taken place. I was still coming to terms with how I felt about it all, but was comforted in the knowledge he had at last found peace and had been laid to rest properly. I would visit one day but for now I would light a candle to remember him by and say a prayer.

Half way up the path I noticed a figure standing by the far wall and stopped to greet him. He raised his cane in acknowledgment, nodded his thanks and with a slight shimmer the ghost of Mr Redmond vanished completely.

The temperature inside the church was a welcome respite from the heat of the day, and I stood for a moment cooling down while my eyes adjusted to the dimness. When I was quite sure I wouldn't bump into things if I moved, I collected a candle and lighting it set it with the others. I stood for a moment watching the flickering flames then moved to sit on a pew at the front. There were already several others sitting in quiet contemplation, no doubt including Father Michael in their prayers. Agnes had informed me his funeral was to be held the next day, presided over by the Archbishop of York, and I had already noticed on the way in the sexton hard at work digging the grave.

Several minutes had passed before I felt the presence of someone sit behind me and lean forward. It was Jocasta.

"I'll be in the meeting room. Come and have a cup of tea with me when you're ready," she whispered.

"All right. Just give me a moment and I'll be along," I whispered back.

In the meeting room I found Jocasta putting the finishing touches to the church flowers for Father Michael's Funeral. Stacked along one wall were numerous wreaths and bouquets expressing the sorrow and heartfelt loss of a man, who although hadn't been at St Mary's long, had become a friend to many.

"Is tea all right or would you prefer coffee?"

"Coffee please."

"I must admit this business nearly put me off tea. Although I've brought my own with me this time. I feel awful about what happened. If I hadn't filched the vicar's stuff, poor Anne and Mrs Fielding would have been fine."

"You can hardly blame yourself, Jocasta. You didn't lace it with poison."

"No, I know but I can't help it."

"Well, in that case let's blame Agnes," I said.

"Why would we do that?"

"Because she was the one who forgot to buy more."

"But that's just silly. It's hardly her fault."

"Just as silly as blaming yourself. It wasn't your fault either."

Jocasta looked at me for a minute then burst out laughing.

"Ella, you have no idea how glad I am we met. Come on, let's go and sit outside in the sunshine."

Once again we moved to the bench where we had sat when I first visited St Mary's. It seemed a lifetime ago, and Jocasta obviously had the same train of thought.

"Gosh, it seems ages since we first sat here. Such has a lot has happened since then. I spoke to Agnes last night by the way, she told me what you'd discussed over lunch. I hope you don't mind?"

"Of course I don't mind, it's hardly a secret now. Besides I expected her to considering how close you are."

"Poor Agnes, my dearest friend and I've treated her abominably. I feel horribly guilty about it."

"Agnes will forgive you, Jocasta. In fact I doubt she thinks there is anything to forgive. She probably thinks the same way I do, that you tried so hard to be someone your husband wanted, you lost sight of who you really are."

"No wonder you're such a good detective. Alfie said something similar actually, how did he put it? Something about the hardened shell I had built around myself being a reaction to my unhappiness, he's terribly intuitive. He was right of course although I shan't use it as an excuse."

"You've seen, Alfie, then?"

"Yes, a couple of days ago."

"Will he be moving back to Briarlea?"

"There's a huge amount to be sorted out before then, not least a divorce and an agreeable settlement, which I confess I am dreading having to go through. But Alfie is hugely supportive, we're just taking it one day at a time and enjoying each moment. If he does come back it won't be as a groom however, I'll never go skulking around like that again. I have well and truly learned that particular lesson."

"Well, if he does return, in whatever capacity, might I make a suggestion?"

"Of course?"

"That you find a new position for your scullery maid, Betty? She is very young and impressionable and thinks herself not only in love with Alfie, but that her feelings are reciprocated. I think it will make things terribly difficult for you and Alfie, if he returns and she is still there. It's not her fault, she had a terrible start in life and was on the receiving end of some awful abuse as you know. But I believe she would benefit from another position where she will have a good mentor. She missed so many of her early life lessons and I worry about what she may become."

To my surprise Jocasta put down her tea cup and enfolded me in a hug.

"Gosh, you're such a good egg, Ella. I'm so glad we're friends, and yes I shall find somewhere perfect for Betty."

Releasing me and reaching for her tea, she went on to ask if there had been any new developments in the case.

"Actually I spoke to Sergeant Baxter this morning and there's a few things come to light that make him believe Mr Redmond wasn't her first victim."

"Good heavens, that's shocking news! Thank goodness you caught her when you did, Ella, it sounds to me as though she would have just carried on marrying and murdering if you hadn't. It's peculiar the way things work out, isn't it? Father Michael knew she was guilty and had wanted to stop her. In his own way, desperately tragic though it was he has done just that."

Chapter TWELVE

TWO DAYS AFTER THE FUNERAL Mrs Shaw and I finished 'The Art of the Lie.'

"It's excellent, isn't it?" she said.

"It really is, Mrs Shaw, we should be jolly proud of ourselves. I can't thank you enough for all your help. I shall of course give you credit on the cover."

"Actually I'd rather you didn't if you don't mind. But I would very much like a copy once it's printed if that's possible?"

"That's more than possible, Mrs Shaw, you deserve it."

We were just packing it up ready to send to Uncle Albert when Mrs Parsons came bustling in, a look of barely suppressed excitement on her face.

"Whatever is the matter, Mrs Parsons?"

"Miss Bridges, Mrs Shaw, I wonder if you have time to come down to the kitchen for a moment?"

"Yes of course. But is something the matter?"

"Not at all, Miss Bridges," she said enigmatically, then bustled off towards the back stairs.

Mrs Shaw and I shared a puzzled glance and then followed.

In the kitchen we found Tom standing to attention with Digger at his side. Everything became clear then and I felt the immediate prick of tears spring unbidden to my eyes.

"Oh, Tom. Is it finished?" I breathed.

He nodded, a huge grin plastered on his face, and reaching into his pocket handed me an enormous wrought iron key. I looked at Mrs Shaw, then at Mrs Parsons, then finally back at Tom.

"Well, what are we waiting for? Let's go!" I said to them all, and raced out into the garden, Digger hot on my heels and the others not far behind.

I ran across the lawns with the exuberance and excitement of a child who had awoken on Christmas morning to find Father Christmas had visited. The weeks since John's telephone call had weighed heavily, as though a huge invisible millstone had been placed around my neck, forcing me to stoop lower and lower until I barely had the strength to lift my head. But with John now at peace and the murder of Father Michael solved, the weight had been lifted. Of course a telephone call barely two hours later would put a stop to all that, but for the moment I felt free and as light as a feather.

I stopped in front of the huge gate and taking a step forward read aloud the engraved plaque which had been placed there.

'To think or reflect is to step aside from events. To give up the world for a space of internal quiet, as if you have entered a walled garden.'

I gently traced the letters with my finger and thought how utterly perfect it was.

"Do the honours then, Miss Bridges," said Mrs Parsons who had come up puffing and panting behind me.

I lifted a shaking hand and inserted the key into the lock. With a clockwise twist I heard a click and slowly pushed open the gate. I stood on the threshold for a moment, then took a step inside.

"Oh, my goodness," whispered Mrs Parsons behind me.

"How splendid," said Mrs Shaw.

It could have been the inspiration for Frances Hodgson Burnett's novel so completely magical was it. I turned to Tom who was waiting in his usual quiet way.

"It's more than I ever dreamed possible, Tom, you have worked miracles here, it's as though we have our own slice of Eden. A simple thank you just doesn't seem enough for the oasis you have created but know I will be forever grateful for what you have done, it's exactly what I need. But please understand, this is as much your garden as it is mine and you must treat it as such."

Tom grinned and nodded, then beckoned for us all to follow and we began to explore in earnest. There were two things I had noticed immediately upon entering, the first was the long greenhouse which ran the entire length of one wall. Freshly painted in dark green with white window frames on an old red brick base, it had two steps leading up to an interior full of everything a gardener could possibly need, and I couldn't wait to begin work.

The second was in the absolute centre of the enormous space, a huge old weeping willow tree whose frond like branches fell to the ground like a living waterfall. It must have been planted many years ago and been growing all this time, just waiting for someone to rediscover it. But the real magic was inside. A secret within a secret.

As I stepped through the leafy curtain into the cool space below I saw attached to the strongest branch a simple rope swing, with a sturdy wooden seat. On the opposite side was an iron table and matching chairs with rose patterned cushions. To the rear of the enormous trunk, suspended between two thick branches, to my delighted surprise was a hammock in a thick and colourful striped fabric, upon which rested several cushions.

"Well, I never," said Mrs Parsons coming up behind me and gazing at the hammock.

I laughed and pushing my way back through the branches went to explore further in the sunshine. There was a huge herb garden in the shape of a cartwheel made from woven willow, and further along several strawberry planters, their luscious red fruits ready for picking. There were rows of tomato plants with marigolds planted between, and I smiled remembering Jocasta's tip which Tom apparently already knew. Along the walls were trained trees, their wares in abundance, three kinds of apples and two sorts of pears. Plums and damsons which would fruit later in the year, and even a medlar, unusual in that it provided its fruit in winter. Various beds showed redcurrant and blackcurrant bushes, alongside blackberries and gooseberries, as well as my favourite raspberries. And further along the large leaf and red stalks of rhubarb were apparent.

Through a magnificent avenue of white rose arches, their branches heavy with creamy white blooms, I discovered an entirely separate section of the garden and was amazed to find a row of beehives. I had been aware of their gentle buzzing in the background, and had watched as they flew from plant to plant feeding on the nectar, but had never thought they were housed here.

"Mr Honeycoat looks after the hives. It's a bit of a specialist job, you see, and Tom prefers to look after the plants. But you need them for pollinating so I asked Mr Honeycoat if he'd help out, everything else was a secret from me though. That's all right, is it?" asked Mrs Shaw.

"Of course it is, Mrs Shaw, it's a wonderful idea. Sorry, did you say Honeycoat? And he keeps bees?" I couldn't keep the smile from my voice but she smiled along with me.

"I rather think he chose his profession to go along with his name, but there's no doubt he knows what he's doing. You'll have jars of fresh honey before you know it. In fact you'll have far more of everything than you'll ever need, Miss Bridges," she said looking around the garden with a frown as it dawned on her just how much food there really was here.

"Yes, I've just come to realise that myself. I also realise Tom will need help if this venture is to be successful. We don't want to waste anything but there's enough here to feed the entire island, and I don't think it's possible to pick, bottle, pickle, bake, cook and eat everything fast enough. I know he can't possibly have done all this work alone too."

"Well, he did do a lot of it and he was in charge. He had a very definite plan of how it was all to be and woe betide anyone who deviated from it. But I confess his brothers did help, and a couple of their friends when it came to the heavier labour, but they are trustworthy types. I knew you wouldn't want strangers traipsing about the place so kept it in the family, as it were."

"Your family is a credit to you, Mrs Parsons, please thank them for me and tell them they are more than welcome to the fruits of their labour whenever they want it. I wonder if you would also help me find some extra staff to work under Tom? Perhaps another two or three, if you have time?"

"You leave it with me, Miss Bridges," she said, then wandered off to inspect the cabbages.

I had barely seen Mrs Shaw since we had entered the garden but she eventually caught up with me by the runner beans, their bright orange flowers already beginning to show.

"Tom has worked absolute wonders in here. You must be very pleased."

"Oh, I am indeed, it's surpassed everything I had hoped for. I've barely had time to look at everything even though we've been here for ages."

"Did you notice the sundial?"

"No I didn't, where is it?"

"Over near the salad beds, it seems to be very old. I also spied some statuary near the potato patch you may want to have a look at."

"I must have missed that too. Is this goodbye by any chance, Mrs Shaw?"

"It is, Miss Bridges."

"Can you not stay for lunch?"

"I'm afraid not, I'm due in London shortly."

"Ah, news of your next assignment?"

She nodded.

"Well, let me walk you back."

And we left Tom and his mother chatting together by the cold-frames, while we returned to the house.

"Will we meet again, do you think?" I asked her as we stood in the hall by the front door.

She paused for a moment.

"If I ever find myself in this neck of the woods, Miss Bridges, I'll be certain to pay you a visit," she said.

I think we both knew it would be highly unlikely but left it at that.

"Well goodbye, Miss Bridges, and best of luck."

"Goodbye, Mrs Shaw, and thank you. For everything."

She turned and was halfway down the path when she stopped and looked back.

"Oh, and while I remember, when it comes the time for you to purchase a motor car, go and see Simpkins, at the garage here. He knows what he's talking about and will get you a good deal."

"I'll do that," I said.

As I waved a final Goodbye to Mrs Shaw I heard the telephone ringing in the hall.

"Hello?"

"Isobella, is that you?"

"Mother?"

"Oh, thank goodness. Listen do you think you could come right away?"

"To France? Yes, of course but what's happened, are you all right?"

"Not really, dear, no. You see I rather think I'm about to be arrested."

Other books in the series

FREE Prequel Book 0 — The Yellow Cottage Mystery

Find out how it all began…

One glimpse was all it took for a child to fall in love with The Yellow Cottage. Years later she returns as an adult to find it's for sale. But not everything is as it seems…

Will she be able to make this the home she's dreamed about for so long, or will the cottage reject her as it has all others before?

The Yellow Cottage Mystery is the short story prequel to the mystery series and tells the tale of how Ella comes to find the cottage and the adoption of her unusual sidekick.

* **This book is available exclusively to those who sign up to become part of my Reader's Group mailing list. I only send emails to let you know of new releases and never send spam.**

You can sign up and get your free book on the website:

www.jnewwrites.com

Book One — An Accidental Murder

When a strange child follows her home on the train from London, Ella Bridges feels bound to help her. However she soon discovers the child is not what she seems.

Having recently moved into a large home on Linhay Island, affectionately known locally as The Yellow Cottage, Ella finds herself at the centre of a murder investigation thanks to a special gift from the previous house owner.

Along with her unusual sidekick, a former cottage resident, Ella follows clues which take her to the heart of London.

As the mystery unravels she is forced to enter the lion's den to solve the crime and stop the perpetrator. But can she do it before she becomes the next victim?

Book Two — The Curse of Arundel Hall

One ghost, one murder, one hundred years apart. But are they connected?

Ella has discovered a secret room in The Yellow Cottage, but with it comes a ghost. Who was she? And how did she die? Ella needs to find the answers before either of them can find peace. But suddenly things take a nasty turn for the worse.

Ella Bridges has been living on Linhay Island for several months but still hasn't discovered the identity of her ghostly guest. Deciding to research the history of her cottage for clues she finds it is connected to Arundel Hall, the large Manor

House on the bluff, and when an invitation to dinner arrives realises it is the perfect opportunity to discover more.

However the evening takes a shocking turn when one of their party is murdered. Is The Curse of Arundel Hall once again rearing its ugly head, or is there a simpler explanation?

Ella suddenly finds herself involved in two mysteries at once, and again joins forces with Scotland Yard's Police Commissioner to try and catch a killer. But will they succeed?

A word about reviews:

Reviews are very important for the success of a book. If you've read and enjoyed any of mine, please leave a review, even if it's just a few words, it really helps. Thank you!

About the Author

J. New has had a lifelong love affair with storytelling in all its forms, so it was only natural that when the opportunity presented itself she would turn to writing books.

Adopted at six weeks old into a loving family, she grew up in a small, picturesque town in West Yorkshire surrounded by nature and with the river Wharfe on her doorstep. Books became her salvation when she found she could 'switch off real life' by immersing herself in the stories, *"I spent a good deal of time either in my own imagination or in someone else's."*

Her choice of genre, British mysteries set in the 1930's, stems from a love of books and films from the era, but the more contemporary ghostly twist originates from personal and family experience.

When not writing she spends her free time with her soulmate, partner and best friend, (luckily they are all the same person), her rescue animals, gardening, drawing or decorating. A vegetarian, she's also an advocate for holistic, natural health products.

You can connect with her on social media at the following places:

FACEBOOK: www.facebook.com/jnewwrites

TWITTER: twitter.com/newwrites

GOODREADS: www.goodreads.com/author/show/7984711.J_New

WEBSITE: www.jnewwrites.com

Printed in Great Britain
by Amazon